TALES OF FAITH & WONDER

TALES OF FAITH & WONDER

STORIES OF

CHRISTIAN FAITH

FROM A

MASTER STORYTELLER

· · · · · · ·

Hans Christian Andersen
ILLUSTRATED BY HAL BETZOLD

Chariot VICTOR
P U B L I S H I N G
A DIVISION OF COOK COMMUNICATIONS

Chariot Victor Publishing
Cook Communications, Colorado Springs, CO 80918
Cook Communications, Paris, Ontario
Kingsway Communications, Eastbourne, England

TALES OF FAITH AND WONDER

These stories have been edited for today's younger readers from an old English translation of Hans Christian Andersen's stories. Every attempt was made to find the name of the translator, without success. To that person we are deeply grateful.

Unless otherwise noted, all Scripture quotations in this publication are from the *Holy Bible, New International Version®*. Copyright ©1973, 1978, 1984 International Bible Society. Used by permission of Zondervan Publishing House. All rights reserved.
Scriptures marked (ICB) are quoted from the *International Children's Bible, New Century Version.* Copyright ©1973, 1986, 1988 by Word Publishing, Dallas, Texas 75039. Used by permission.

Compiled, edited, and adapted by Elisabeth Brown, Karl Schaller, and Julie Smith
Cover design by Ragont Design Studio
Design Manager, Brenda Franklin
Cover illustration by Hal Betzold
First printing, 1997
Printed in Canada
01 99 98 97   5 4 3 2 1

ISBN: 0-7814-0192-5

Library of Congress Cataloging-in-Publication Data
Andersen, H.C. (Hans Christian), 1805-1875.
  [Tales. English. Selections]
  Tales of faith and wonder / by Hans Christian Andersen.
    p. cm.
  Summary: Presents twenty-one fairy tales, including "Thumbelina," "The Ugly Duckling,"
"The Lovliest Rose in the World," and "Hidden Is Not Forgotten," with Christian commentary.
    ISBN 0-7814-0192-5
    1. Fairy Tales—Denmark. 2. Children's Stories, Danish—Translations into English.
    [1. Fairy Tales. 2. Short Stories.]
    I. Title.
  IN PROCESS   96-22429
  [Fic]—dc20   CIP
                                                    AC

TABLE OF CONTENTS

FOREWORD

The Lord blessed me with many wonderful things in my childhood: Christian parents, two younger sisters, a loving extended family with aunts, uncles, and cousins galore, and books. Being a natural introvert surrounded by all those people, I naturally took to my room and spent hours with the books. I remember two in particular: the first, *A Child's Bible Reader,* which taught me the stories of the Bible, and *The Tales of Hans Christian Andersen,* which taught me to dream and fly upon wings of fantasy. Those two books, my favorites, did not seem at all oppposite. I figured that the same God who enabled a boy to kill a giant with a slingshot could also inspire tales of a kind and tiny maid who lived in a flower.

Early on I learned that there were three kinds of literature: nonfiction, fiction, and the Holy Bible, so sacred and true that it deserves its own category. I've had some parents tell me that they hesitate to share fiction with their children because "they might confuse the Bible with fairy tales" or "because fiction isn't true."

Let me assure you—because I had been taught that the Bible was God's Holy Word, I wasn't any more apt to confuse the Holy Spirit with Cinderella's Fairy Godmother than I would confuse my mother with my Aunts Edna, Irene or Ruby. I just knew the difference. And while fiction stories aren't true, the emotions within them certainly are. A child who reads and experiences Andersen's "The Little Mermaid" doesn't come away believing that merpeople live at the bottom of the sea, but she does believe in the mermaid's sacrificial love.

Plato once said, "We ought to esteem it of the greatest importance that the fictions which children first hear should be adapted in the most perfect manner to the promotion of virtue." The tales in this book promote the virtues of godliness through fictional stories. Though they are fanciful, they speak of honest emotion and exalt the goodness of God. Perhaps the tales of Hans Christian Andersen speak so powerfully to children because he does not gloss over or deny real suffering, pain, or loneliness. Poor John of "The Traveling Companion" weeps because "he had no one in the world, neither father nor mother, neither sister nor brother." The loving little mermaid (unlike the Disney adaptation) surrenders her voice, her love, and her life for the prince she adores. Elisa, sister to the wild swans, suffers great pain and fear as she weaves the stinging nettles into coats, and she is nearly burnt at the stake before she is vindicated.

But love and hope always triumph. The Ugly Duckling humbly realizes that his Creator made him the most beautiful of swans, the lowly little pea inspires an invalid girl to live, and from the spilled blood of Christ at Calvary blooms the loveliest rose in the world.

Hans Christian Andersen experienced perhaps more than his share of disappointment and suffering in his lifetime, but his vibrant faith enabled him to find light in the darkness and hope in despair. Born in Denmark in 1805, Andersen tried careers in singing, acting, and novel writing before he settled into his gift as a storyteller. He never married, but did suffer an unrequited love, hence the tender theme that sustains "The Little Mermaid."

In the last two hundred years his fanciful tales have become a part of the fabric of childhood, for what child has not giggled at the silliness of "The Emperor's New Clothes" or been encouraged by "The Ugly Duckling"? Andersen himself, who attended a Copenhagen grammar school at a later age than most of the other boys, was taunted for his big size, his long nose, and his close-set eyes. He was the ugly duckling, but what a lovely swan he became!

Andersen has sketched a variety of fictional worlds: some funny, some bittersweet, some sentimental. With your sons and daughters, I hope you enjoy them all as much as I did. Curl up together, turn off the television, let the phone ring. And step together into the delightful worlds of Hans Christian Andersen.

Angela Elwell Hunt
Seminole, Florida, 1996

A NOTE FROM THE EDITOR:

Because these stories are from a very old English translation, we felt it necessary to edit them for today's young readers. This means only that we have tried to remain faithful to Andersen's original Danish text. Old English words and phrases have been changed to be easily understood by today's children. Andersen himself "took great pains not to use words which [children] might have difficulty understanding," according to biographer Elias Bredsdorff. He also used a very informal style that was like the contemporary spoken language instead of what was considered "good writing" at the time.

My sincere and undying thanks are due to Elias Bredsdorff for his excellent biography, *Hans Christian Andersen, The Story of His Life and Work*, and to Erik Christian Haugaard for his current English translation, *The Complete Fairy Tales and Stories*, which was an invaluable help.

EJB

ILLUSTRATOR'S ACKNOWLEDGMENTS

The illustrator would like to thank the following family and friends who served as models. They generously gave of their time and spirit and brought the characters in these pages to life:

Rich Berg, Nick and Eileen Betzold, Nick, Cheryl, Nicky, Sarah, and Carly Betzold, Huntley Brown, Mike Coogan, Brad Heitman, Eric Johnson, Peter and Kay Jung, Dawn Lauck, Paula Moore, Harry Newman, Andree Novander, Patrick, Diana, Ryan, and Ricky Sheahan, Annette Smaga, Ken, Joyce, Rebecca, Rachel, Joel, and Sarah Story, and Joshua Trob. Thanks also to the staff at the Jacob Henry Mansion in Joliet, Illinois, for allowing the illustrator to photograph the estate. Special thanks to a friend in Christ—hidden is not forgotten.

My gift to the world.
HCA

To the Hendricks Family,
who taught me "What the Whole Family Said."
EJB

To my wife, Linda, and our children, Amber and Beau, with my love.
I am thankful for their love and support.
And as the poet so wisely wrote with the foolish pen and inkstand,
"We are only the instruments which the Almighty uses;
to Him alone be the honor."
HMB

WHAT THE
WHOLE FAMILY SAID

*"Now choose life, so that you and your
children may live and that you may love the LORD
your God, listen to his voice, and hold fast to him.
For the LORD is your life, and he will give you
many years in the land he swore to give to
your fathers Abraham, Isaac and Jacob."
(Deuteronomy 30:19-20)*

hat did the whole family say? Well, let's listen first to what little Mary said.

It was little Mary's birthday, the loveliest of all days, she thought. All her little friends came to play with her, and she wore the most beautiful dress. She had gotten it from her grandmother, who was now with the good Lord, but Grandmother herself had cut and sewed it before she went up into the bright, beautiful heaven. The table in Mary's room shone with presents. There was the neatest little toy kitchen, with all that belongs to a kitchen, and a doll which could roll its eyes and say "Mama" when one pressed its stomach. There was also a picture book with the loveliest stories to read, if one could read! But it was nicer than any story to live through many birthdays.

"Yes, it is lovely to live," said little Mary. Grandfather added that life was the loveliest fairy tale.

In the room close by were Mary's two brothers; they were big boys, the one nine years old, the other eleven. They also thought it was lovely to be alive, to live in their way. Not to be a child like Mary, but to be smart schoolboys, to have "excellent" on their report cards, and to be able to enjoy a game with their friends, to skate in winter, and to ride bicycles in summer, to read about castles, drawbridges, and prisons, and to hear about discoveries all over the world.

These children lived and played on the ground floor. Up above lived another family, also with children, but these were grown-up. The one son was seventeen years old, the second twenty, but the third was very old, little Mary said—he was twenty-five and engaged.

They were all very happy, had good parents, good clothes, good abilities, and they knew what they wanted. "Forward! Away with old fences! We want to see the world! That is the most wonderful thing we know. It's true; life is the loveliest fairy tale!"

Father and Mother, both elderly people—naturally they must be older than the children—said with a smile on their lips, with a smile in their eyes and heart, "How young they are, the young people! Things do not go quite as they think in the world, but they do go. Life is a strange, lovely fairy tale."

Overhead, a little nearer heaven, as one says, in the attic, lived Grandfather. He was old, but so young in spirit, always cheerful, and he could also tell stories, many and long. He had traveled widely, and lovely things from all the countries in the world stood in his room. There were pictures from floor to ceiling. It always smelled of flowers here, even in winter, and then a big fire burned in the fireplace. It was so nice to sit and look into it and hear how it crackled and sputtered. "It repeats old memories to me," said Grandfather, and to little Mary it seemed as if many pictures showed themselves in the fire.

But in the big bookcase close by stood the real books. One of these Grandfather read very often, and he called it the Book of Books; it was the Bible. There in pictures was shown the whole history of man and of the world, the Creation, the Flood, the Kings, and the King of kings.

"All that has happened and will happen stands in this book!" said Grandfather. "So very much in such a little book! Think of it! Everything that a man has to pray for is said and put in a few words in the Lord's Prayer. It is a drop of grace, a pearl of comfort from God. Little child, keep it carefully! Never lose it, however big you grow, and then you will not be left alone on the changing paths of life! God's Word will shine in on you and you will not be lost."

Grandfather's eyes shone at that; they beamed with joy. Once in earlier days they had wept, "and that was also good," he said. "It was a time of trial when things looked gray. Now I have sunshine about me and in me. The older one grows, the better one sees, both in good times and bad times, that our Father is always with us. Life is the loveliest fairy tale. Only God can give us that, and it lasts into eternity."

"It is lovely to live," said little Mary.

The little and the big boys said so too; Father and Mother and the whole family said it.

But above all lived Grandfather, and he had experience; he was the oldest of them all. He knew all the stories, all the fairy tales, and he said right out of his heart, "Life is the loveliest fairy tale!"

THE PEN AND THE INKSTAND

We are often proud of our accomplishments, but Jesus reminds us in John 15:5, " . . . apart from me you can do nothing." Hans Christian Andersen knew firsthand about fame and glory, but he still said, "If what I have accomplished has any value, the honor is God's alone!"

T he Inkstand stood upon the table in the room of a poet. He heard someone say, "It is wonderful what can come out of an inkstand—such a little pot of ink. What will the next thing be? It is wonderful!"

"Yes, certainly," said the Inkstand. "No one can understand it—that's what I always say," he exclaimed to the Pen and to the other articles on the table that could hear. "It is wonderful what a number of things can come out of me. It's quite incredible. And I really don't even know myself what will come next, when that man begins to dip into me. One drop out of me is enough for half a page of paper. From me all the works of the poet go forth—all these imaginary people—all the deep feelings, the humor, the vivid pictures of nature. From me all these things have come forth, and from me proceed the charming maidens, and brave knights on prancing steeds, and all the lame and the blind, and I don't know what else—I assure you I don't think of anything."

"There you are right," said the Pen. "You don't think at all, for if you did, you would understand that you are only fluid. You give the fluid so that I may write on the paper what I think. It is the pen that writes. No man doubts that. Indeed, most people know more about poetry than an old inkstand."

"You haven't had much experience," replied the Inkstand.

"Inkpot!" exclaimed the Pen.

Late in the evening the poet came home. He had been to a concert, where he had heard a famous violinist, and had been enchanted by what he had heard. The player had drawn so many sounds from the instrument: sometimes it had sounded like tinkling water drops, like rolling pearls, sometimes like birds twittering in chorus, and then again it went on like the wind through the fir trees.

It seemed to the poet as though not only the strings made the music, but every part of the instrument. It was a wonderful performance, and even though it was a difficult piece to play, the musician made it look as though anyone might do it. The violin sang by itself, and the bow moved by itself—those two seemed to do everything. The audience forgot the master who guided them and breathed soul and spirit into them. The master was forgotten, but the poet remembered him, and named him, and wrote down his thoughts about the evening.

"How foolish it would be for the violin and the bow to boast of their greatness! And yet, we men often do the same foolish thing— the poet, the artist, the scientist, the general—we all do it. We are only the instruments which the Almighty uses. He alone deserves the honor! We have nothing to be proud of."

Yet as he wrote down those very thoughts, the Pen and Inkstand continued to argue.

"Did you not hear him read aloud what I have written down?" said the Pen.

"Yes, what I gave you to write," retorted the Inkstand.

"Ink tub!" cried the Pen.

"Writing stick!" cried the Inkstand.

That night, the poet could not sleep. Thoughts welled up from within him, like the tones from the violin, falling like pearls, rushing like the storm wind through the forests. He felt his own heart in these thoughts, and caught a ray from the Eternal Master.

To *Him* be all the honor!

FIVE OUT OF ONE POD

Even things that come from the same place can end up very differently. Jesus told a story like this one about seeds thrown by a farmer. "But the one who received the seed that fell on good soil is the man who hears the word and understands it. He produces a crop, yielding a hundred, sixty, or thirty times what was sown." (Matthew 13:23)

here were five Peas in one pod. They were green, and the pod was green, and so they thought the whole world was green. The pod grew, and the Peas grew; they each made themselves at home. The sun shone outside and warmed the pod, and the rain made it clear and transparent. And the Peas as they sat there became bigger and bigger, and more and more thoughtful, for they had to pass the time doing something.

"Are we to sit here forever?" asked one. "I'm afraid we shall become hard by sitting so long. It seems to me there must be something outside—I have an idea what it might be like."

And weeks went by. Suddenly the Peas felt a tug at the pod. It was torn off, passed through human hands, and glided down into the pocket of a jacket, in company with other full pods.

"Now we shall be opened!" they said.

"I should like to know who of us will get farthest!" said the smallest of the five. "Yes, now we will soon find out."

"What is to be will be," said the biggest.

"*Crack!*" The pod burst, and all five Peas rolled out into the bright sunshine. There they lay in a child's hand. A little boy was clutching the pod, and said they were fine peas for his peashooter. He put one in at once and shot it out.

"Now I'm flying out into the wide world; catch me if you can!" And he was gone.

"I," said the second, "shall fly straight into the sun. That's a pod worth looking at, and one that exactly suits me." And away he went.

The next two Peas said, "We can sleep where we land." They were put into the peashooter. "We shall go farthest," they said.

"What is to happen will happen," said the last, as he was shot forth

out of the peashooter. He flew up against a rotten board under the attic window, into a crack which was filled up with moss and soft dirt. Moss closed round him, and there he lay, a prisoner, but not forgotten by our Lord.

Within, in the little attic, lived a poor woman, who went out in the day to clean stoves, saw wood, and to do other hard work, for she was strong and industrious. But she always remained poor, and at home in the attic lay her half-grown only daughter, who was very delicate and weak. For a whole year she had stayed in bed.

The little girl lay patiently all day long while her mother went out to earn money. It was spring, and early in the morning, just as the mother was about to go out to work, the sun shone mildly and pleasantly through the little window and threw its rays across the floor. The sick girl fixed her eyes on the lowest pane in the window.

"What is that green thing that looks in at the window? It is moving in the wind."

The mother stepped to the window and half opened it. "Oh!" said she, "on my word, it is a little pea which has taken root here and is putting out its little leaves. How could it have got here into the crack? Now you have a little garden to look at."

The sick girl's bed was moved nearer to the window, so she could always see the growing pea, and the mother went forth to her work.

"Mother, I think I shall get well," said the sick child in the evening. "The sun shone in upon me today delightfully warm. The little pea is doing well, and I shall do well too. I'll get up and go out into the warm sunshine."

"God grant it!" said the mother.

And so the little Pea did shoot up—one could see how it grew every day.

"Look, here is a flower coming!" said the woman one day. And now she began to cherish the hope that her sick daughter would recover. A week afterwards, the invalid for the first time sat up for a whole hour. Quite happy, she sat there in the warm sunshine; the window was opened, and in front of it outside stood a pink pea blossom, fully blown. The sick girl bent down and gently kissed the delicate leaves.

"The Heavenly Father Himself has planted that pea and caused it to grow, to be a joy to you, and to me, also, my dear child!" said the glad mother.

But what about the other Peas? Why, the one who flew out into the wide world and said, "Catch me if you can," found a home in a pigeon's stomach. The two lazy ones got just as far, for they, too, were eaten up by pigeons. And the fourth, who wanted to go up into the sun, fell into the gutter.

But the young girl at the attic window stood with gleaming eyes, the hue of health on her cheeks, and folded her thin hands over the pea blossom, and thanked God for it.

THE LITTLE MERMAID

Even humans can learn a lot from this little mermaid who followed her heart and didn't betray her true love. "The Lord will reward everyone for whatever good he does, whether he is slave or free." (Ephesians 6:8)

ar out in the sea the water is as blue as the petals of the most beautiful cornflower and as clear as the purest glass. Deep beneath the surface of the blue waters live the sea people.

In the deepest spot of all lies the Sea King's castle: the walls are of coral, and the tall, pointed windows of the clearest amber. Mussel shells form the roof, and they open and shut according as the water flows. It looks lovely, for in each shell lie gleaming pearls, a single one of which would be a great ornament in a queen's crown.

The Sea King had been a widower for many years, while his old mother kept house for him. The Sea King's mother was very fond of her granddaughters, the little sea princesses. These were six pretty children, but the youngest was the most beautiful of all. Her skin was as clear and as fine as a rose leaf; her eyes were as blue as the deepest sea, but, like all the rest, she had no feet, for her body ended in a fish tail.

The Little Mermaid was a strange child, quiet and thoughtful. When the other sisters made a display of the beautiful things they had received out of wrecked ships, she would have nothing beyond the red sea flowers which resembled the sun, except a pretty marble statue. This was a figure of a charming boy, hewn out of white clear stone, which had sunk down to the bottom of the sea from a wreck.

There was no greater pleasure for the Little Mermaid than to hear of the world of men above them. The old Grandmother had to tell all she knew of ships and towns, of men and animals. It seemed to the Little Mermaid particularly beautiful that up on the earth the flowers shed fragrance, for they had none down at the bottom of the sea.

"When you are eighteen years old," said the Grandmother, "you may rise up out of the sea and sit on the rocks in the moonlight and see the great ships sailing by. Then you will see forests and towns!"

Year after year, the Little Mermaid often looked up through the dark blue water at the world above and wondered.

* * * * *

At last the Little Mermaid was really eighteen years old.

"Now, you see, you are grown up," said the Grandmother.

"Farewell, Grandmother!" she said, and then the Mermaid rose, light and clear as a water bubble, up through the sea.

The sun had just set when she lifted her head above the sea, but all the clouds still shone like roses and gold, and in the pale red sky the evening star gleamed bright and beautiful. The air was mild and fresh and the sea quite calm. There lay a great ship with

three masts. One single sail only was set, for not a breeze stirred, and around in the shrouds and on the yards sat the sailors. There was music and singing, and as the evening closed in, hundreds of colored lanterns were lighted up and it looked as if the flags of every nation were waving in the air.

The Little Mermaid

swam straight to the cabin window, and each time the sea lifted her up she could look through the panes, which were clear as crystal, and see many people standing within dressed in their best. But the handsomest of all was the young Prince with the great black eyes. He was certainly not much more than nineteen years old; it was his birthday, and that was the cause of all this festivity.

The sailors were dancing up on deck, and when the young Prince came out, more than a hundred rockets rose into the air; they shone like day, so that the Little Mermaid was quite startled, and dived under the water. But soon she put out her head again, and then it seemed just as if all the stars of heaven were falling down upon her. She had never seen such fireworks.

It became late, but the Little Mermaid could not turn her eyes from the ship and from the beautiful Prince. The colored lanterns were extinguished, rockets ceased to fly into the air, and no more cannons were fired. The ship began to move faster, and one sail after another was spread.

Now the waves rose higher, great clouds came up, and in the distance there was lightning. Oh! It was going to be fearful weather, therefore the sailors furled the sails. The great ship flew over the wild sea. The waters rose up like great black mountains which wanted to roll over the masts, but like a swan the ship dived into the valleys between these high waves and then let itself be lifted on high again.

To the Little Mermaid this seemed merry sport, but to the sailors it appeared very differently. The sea broke into the ship, the mainmast snapped in two like a thin reed, and the ship lay over on her side, while water rushed into the hold. Now the Little Mermaid saw that the people were in peril.

One moment it was so pitch dark that not a single object could be seen, but when it lightened it became so bright that she could distinguish everyone on board. Every one was doing the best he could for himself. She looked particularly for the young Prince, and when the ship parted she saw him sink into the sea. At first she was very glad, for now he would come down to her. But then she remembered that people could not live in the water, and that when he got down to her father's palace he would certainly be dead. No, he must not die.

So she swam about among the beams and planks that strewed the surface, quite forgetting that one of them might have crushed her. Diving down deep under the water, she again rose high up among the waves, and in this way she at last came to the Prince. His arms and legs began to fail him, his beautiful eyes closed, and he would have died had the Little Mermaid not come. She held his head up over the water and then allowed the waves to carry them both toward shore.

When the morning came, the storm had passed by. Of the ship not a fragment was to be seen. The sun came up red and shining out of the water. It was as if its beams brought back life to the cheeks of the Prince, but his eyes remained closed. The Mermaid kissed his high fair forehead and put back his wet hair, and he seemed to her to be like the marble statue in her little garden. She kissed him again and hoped that he might live.

She saw in front of her the dry land and high blue mountains where the white snow gleamed. On the coast were glorious green forests, and a church stood there, at the edge of a little bay. She swam with the handsome Prince straight toward the rock where the fine white sand had been cast up. There she laid him upon the sand, taking special care that his head was raised in the warm sunshine.

Now all the bells rang in the great white church, and many young girls came walking through the garden. The Little Mermaid swam farther out between some high stones that stood up out of the water, laid some sea foam upon her hair and neck, so that no one could see her little face, and then she watched to see who would come to the poor Prince.

In a short time a young girl went that way. She seemed very startled, but only for a moment; then she brought more people, and the Mermaid saw the Prince come back to life and smile at all around him. But he did not cast a smile at her; he did not know that she had saved him. She felt very sorrowful, and when he was taken away into the church's great buildings, she dived sadly under the water and returned to her father's palace.

She had always been gentle and quiet, but now she became much more so. Her sisters asked what she had seen the first time she rose to the surface, but she would tell them nothing.

*   *   *   *   *

Many an evening and many a morning she went up to the place where she had left the Prince. At last she could endure it no longer and told all to one of her sisters. Then the others heard of it too, but nobody knew of it beyond these and a few other mermaids. One of these knew who the Prince was; she, too, had seen the festival on board the ship, and she told them where his kingdom lay.

"Come, little sister!" said the other princesses, and, linking their arms together, they rose up in a long row out of the sea at the place where they knew the Prince's palace stood.

This palace was built of a kind of bright yellow stone, with great marble staircases, one of which led directly down into the sea. Over the roof rose splendid golden cupolas, and between the pillars which surrounded the whole dwelling stood marble statues which looked as if they were alive. Through the clear glass in the high windows one looked into the glorious halls.

Now she knew where the Prince lived, and many an evening and many a night she spent there on the water. She swam far closer to the land than any of the others would have dared to venture. In fact, she went right up the narrow channel under the splendid marble balcony, which threw a broad shadow upon the water. Here she sat and watched the young Prince, who thought himself quite alone in the bright moonlight.

Many an evening she saw him sailing, amid the sounds of music, in his costly boat with the waving flags.

More and more the Little Mermaid began to love mankind, and more and more she wanted to wander about among those whose world seemed far larger than her own. There was much she wished to know, but her sisters could not answer all her questions. Therefore, she went to the old Grandmother, because the old lady knew the upper world very well.

"If people do not drown," asked the Little Mermaid, "can they live forever? Or do they die as we die down here in the sea?"

"Yes," replied the old lady, "they, too, must die, and their life is even shorter than ours. We can live to be three hundred years old, but when we cease to exist here, we are turned into foam on the surface of the water, and have not even a grave down here among those we love. We do not have an immortal soul; we never receive another life. We are like the green seaweed, which can never bloom again after it is cut. But human beings have a soul which lives forever, which lives on after the body has become dust; it can mount up through the clear air, up to all the shining stars! As we rise up out of the waters and behold all the lands of the earth, so they can rise up to unknown glorious places which we can never see."

"Why did we not receive an immortal soul?" asked the Little Mermaid, sorrowfully. "I would gladly give all the hundreds of years I have to live to be a human being for only one day, and to have a hope of seeing the heavenly kingdom."

"You must not think of that," replied the old lady.

"Then I will die and float as foam upon the sea, not hearing the music of the waves, nor seeing the pretty flowers and the red sun? I cannot do anything to win an immortal soul?"

"No!" answered the Grandmother. "Only if a man were to love you so that you should be more to him than father or mother. If he should cling to you with his every thought and with all his love, and let the priest lay his right hand in yours with a promise of faithfulness here and in all eternity, then his soul would be joined to your body, and you would receive some of the happiness of mankind. He would give a soul to you and yet retain his own. But that can never happen. What is considered beautiful here in the sea—the fish tail—they would consider ugly on the earth. They don't understand it; there, one must have two clumsy supports which they call legs to be called beautiful."

Then the Little Mermaid sighed, and looked sadly upon her fish tail.

"Let us be glad!" said the old lady. "Let us dance and leap in the three hundred years we have to live. That is certainly long enough. After that we can rest ourselves all the better."

Later the Little Mermaid sat very sad and alone in her garden. She heard the bugle horn sounding through the waters and thought, "Now the Prince is certainly sailing above, he whom I love more than father or mother, he whom I wish for every day, and to whom I could entrust my life's happiness. I will dare everything to win him and an immortal soul. I must go to the Sea Hag, though she has always scared me. Perhaps she can tell me what to do."

*   *   *   *

Now the Little Mermaid went out of her garden to the foaming whirlpools that lay before the Sea Hag's home. She had never traveled that way before. No flowers grew there, no sea grass; only the bare grey sand stretched out toward the whirlpools, where the water rushed round into the deep. She had to pass through these rushing whirlpools to get to the Sea Hag because there was no other road except the one which led over warm bubbling mud. Behind it lay the Sea Hag's house in the midst of an unusual forest. In this forest all the trees and bushes looked like hundred-headed snakes growing up out of the earth. All the branches were long, slimy arms, with fingers like worms, and they moved joint by joint from the root to the farthest point. Anything they could grab in the water they held onto and never let go. The Little Mermaid stopped in front of them quite frightened. Her heart beat with fear and she nearly turned back, but then she thought of the Prince and the human soul, and her courage came back again.

She bound her long flying hair closely around her head, so that the creatures could not seize it. She put her hands together on her breast and then shot forward as a fish shoots through the water, among the worm-like plants, which stretched out their supple arms and fingers after her.

Now she came to a great marshy place in the wood, where fat eels rolled about, showing their ugly yellow bodies. In the midst of this marsh was the Sea Hag's house.

"I know what you want," said the Sea Hag. "It is stupid of you, but you shall have your way, for it will bring you grief, my pretty princess. You want to get rid of your fish tail and have two supports instead of it, like the people of the earth walk with. Then the young Prince may fall in love with you, and you may get him and an immortal soul."

With this the Sea Hag laughed loudly and disagreeably, so that the eels tumbled down to the ground, where they crawled about. "You have come just in time," said the Sea Hag. "After tomorrow at sunrise, I could not have helped you until another year had gone by. I will prepare a drink for you, which you must take to land tomorrow before the sun rises. Seat yourself there and drink it; then your tail will part in two and shrink in and become what the people of the earth call beautiful legs. But it will hurt you—it will seem as if you were cut with a sharp sword. All who see you will declare you to be the prettiest human being they ever beheld. You will keep your graceful walk; no dancer will be able to move so lightly as you. But every step you take will be as if you were walking on sharp knives, and as if you were bleeding. If you will bear all this, I can help you."

"Yes!" said the Little Mermaid, with a trembling voice.

"But, remember," said the Sea Hag, "when you have once received a human form, you can never be a mermaid again. You can never return to your sisters or to your father's palace. And if you do not win the Prince's love, so that he forgets father and mother for your sake, and tells the priest to join your hands, you will not receive an immortal soul. On the first morning after he has married another, your heart will break and you will become foam on the water."

"I will do it," said the Little Mermaid, and her face was as pale as death.

"But you must pay me too," said the Sea Hag. "And it is not a trifle that I ask. You have the finest voice of all; with that you think to enchant him. But this voice you must give to me. The best thing you possess I will have!"

"But if you take away my voice," said the Little Mermaid, "what will I have left?"

"Your beautiful form," replied the Sea Hag, "your graceful walk, and your eloquent eyes; with those you can surely capture a human heart. Well, have you lost your courage?"

"Let it be so," said the Little Mermaid.

And the Sea Hag put on her pot to brew the potion.

*　*　*　*　*

The sun had not yet risen when she saw the Prince's castle and sat on the splendid marble staircase. The moon shone beautifully clear. The Little Mermaid drank the burning potion, and it seemed as if a sharp two-edged sword went through her delicate body. She fell down in a faint and lay as if she were dead. When the sun shone out over the sea, she awoke, and felt a sharp pain, but just before her stood the handsome young Prince. He fixed his coal-black eyes upon her, so that she cast down her own, and then she saw that her fish tail was gone, and that she had the prettiest pair of feet a girl could have. But she had no clothes, so she covered herself in her long hair.

The Prince asked who she was and how she had come there. She looked at him mildly, but very sadly, with her dark blue eyes, for she could not speak. Then he took her by the hand, and led her into the castle. Each step she took was as the Sea Hag had told her—as if she were walking on pointed needles and sharp knives—but she bore it gladly. At the Prince's right hand, she moved on, light as a soap bubble, and he was astonished at her graceful, swaying movements.

She now received splendid clothes of silk and muslin. In the castle she was the most beautiful of all, but she was mute and could neither sing nor speak.

Often lovely slaves would sing before the Prince and his royal parents. One sang more charmingly than all the rest, and the Prince smiled at her and clapped his hands. Then the Little Mermaid became sad; she knew that she herself had once sung far

more sweetly. She thought, "Oh! If only he could know that I have given away my voice forever to be with him."

Now the slaves danced pretty waving dances to the loveliest music. And the Little Mermaid lifted her beautiful arms, stood on the tips of her toes, and glided dancing over the floor as no one had yet danced. All were delighted, and especially the Prince, who called her his little foundling. The Prince said that she should always remain with him, and she received permission to sleep on a velvet cushion before his door.

Day by day, the Prince grew more fond of the Little Mermaid. He loved her as one loves a dear child, but it never came into his head to make her his wife. Yet she had to become his wife, or she would not receive an immortal soul, and would have to become foam on the sea on his wedding morning.

"Do you not love me best of them all?" the eyes of the Little Mermaid seemed to say to the Prince.

"Yes, you are the dearest to me!" said the Prince. "For you have the best heart of them all. You are the most devoted to me, and are like a young girl whom I once saw, but whom I shall not find again. I was on board a ship which was wrecked. The waves threw me ashore near a temple, where several young girls were living. The youngest of them found me by the shore and saved my life. I only saw her twice; she is the only one in the world I could love, but you chase her picture out of my mind, you are so like her. But she belongs to the temple, and therefore my good fortune has sent you to me. We will never part!"

"Ah! He does not know that I saved his life," thought the Little Mermaid. "I carried him over the sea to the wood where the temple stands. I swam under the foam and looked to see if anyone would come. I saw the beautiful girl whom he loves better than me." The Mermaid sighed deeply—she could not weep.

*　　*　　*　　*　　*

But now it was said that the Prince was to marry the beautiful daughter of a neighboring king. A beautiful ship was being prepared and the story was that the Prince traveled to visit the neighboring country. But everyone knew he was really going to see the king's daughter. A great company was to go with him. The Little Mermaid shook her head and smiled, for she knew the Prince's thoughts far better than any of the others.

"I must travel," he had said to her. "I must see the beautiful Princess because my parents desire it, but they will not make me bring her home as my bride. I cannot love her. She is not like the beautiful maiden in the temple, whom you resemble. If I were to choose a bride, I would rather choose you, my dear mute foundling with the speaking eyes."

The next morning the ship sailed into the harbor of the neighboring king's splendid city. All the church bells sounded, and from the high towers the trumpets were blown, while the soldiers stood there with flying colors and flashing bayonets. Each day brought some festivity with it; balls and entertainments followed on another, but the Princess was not yet there. People said she was being educated in a holy temple far away, where she was learning every royal virtue. At last she arrived.

The Little Mermaid was anxious to see the beauty of the Princess. A more lovely vision she had never seen. The Princess's skin was pure and clear, and behind the long dark eyelashes there smiled a pair of faithful dark blue eyes.

"You are the lady who saved me when I lay like a corpse upon the shore," said the Prince. And he folded his blushing bride to his heart. "Oh, I am so happy!" he cried to the Little Mermaid. "The best hope I could have is fulfilled. You will rejoice at my happiness, for you are the most devoted to me of them all!"

The Little Mermaid kissed his hand, and it seemed to her that her heart was broken already.

All the church bells were ringing, and heralds rode about the streets announcing the engagement. On every altar fragrant oil was burning in gorgeous lamps of silver. Bride and bridegroom stood hand in hand and received the bishop's blessing. The Little Mermaid was dressed in cloth of gold and held up the bride's train. But her ears heard nothing of the festive music, her eyes did not see the holy ceremony; she thought of the night of her death, and of all that she had lost in this world.

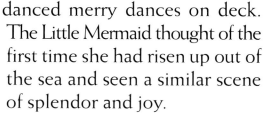

On the same evening the bride and bridegroom went on board the ship. The cannon roared and all the flags waved. The sails swelled in the wind and the ship glided smoothly and lightly over the clear sea. When it grew dark, colored lamps were lighted and the sailors

danced merry dances on deck. The Little Mermaid thought of the first time she had risen up out of the sea and seen a similar scene of splendor and joy.

She knew this was the last evening she would see him for whom she had left her friends and her home, and had given up her beautiful voice. Everlasting night without thought or dream awaited her, for she had no soul, and could win none.

It became quiet on the ship; only the helmsman stood by the helm. The Little Mermaid leaned her arms upon the railing and gazed out toward the east for the morning dawn—the first ray, she knew, would kill her. Then she saw her sisters rising out of the waves.

"The Sea Hag has given us a knife; here it is—look! How sharp! Before the sun rises you must thrust it into the heart of the Prince. You will become a mermaid again, and come back to us, and live your three hundred years before you become dead salt sea foam. Hurry! He or you must die before the sun rises! Kill the Prince and come back! Do you see that red streak in the sky? In a few minutes the sun will rise, and you must die!"

The mermaids vanished beneath the waves.

The Little Mermaid drew back the purple curtain from the tent and saw the beautiful bride lying with her head on the Prince's breast. She bent down and kissed his brow and gazed up to the sky where the morning red was gleaming brighter and brighter. Then she looked at the sharp knife and again fixed her eyes upon the Prince, who in his sleep murmured his bride's name. She only was in his thoughts, and the knife trembled in the Mermaid's hands. But then she flung it far away into the waves. Once more she looked with half-closed eyes upon the Prince; then she threw herself from the ship into the sea, and felt her frame dissolving into foam.

Now the sun rose up out of the sea. The rays fell mild and warm upon the cold sea foam, and the Little Mermaid felt nothing of death. She saw the bright sun, and over her head sailed hundreds of glorious angels. She could see them through the white sails of the ship and the red clouds of the sky. Their speech was melody, but of such a spiritual kind that no human ear could hear it, just as no earthly eye could see them; without wings they floated through the air. The Little Mermaid found that she had a frame like these and was rising more and more out of the foam.

"Where am I going?" she asked, and her voice sounded so spiritual that no earthly music could be compared to it.

"Come away with us!" replied the others. "A mermaid has no immortal soul, and can never gain one, except she win the love of a mortal. Her eternal existence depends upon the power of another. But you, poor Little Mermaid, have pursued with your whole heart the love of the Prince. And because you have shown such selfless love as to sacrifice your life for his, God has granted your desire for an eternal soul."

The Little Mermaid lifted her bright arms toward God's sun, and for the first time she felt tears. On the ship there was again life and noise. She saw the Prince and his bride searching for her; then they looked sadly at the pearly foam, as if they knew that she had thrown herself into the waves. Invisible, she kissed the forehead of the bride, smiled to the Prince, and mounted with the other children of the air on the rosy cloud which floated through the sky.

THE EMPEROR'S NEW CLOTHES

This familiar story is often used to encourage truthfulness. But there is another hidden lesson in it as well. The people in this story are not necessarily great liars, but only too proud to admit they might be less than they think they are. Sometimes a little humility will bring out the truth, ". . . and the truth will set you free." (John 8:32)

any years ago there lived an Emperor who cared so enormously for beautiful new clothes that he spent all his money on them. He had a coat for every hour of the day, and just as they say of a king, "He is in council," one always said of him, "The Emperor is in the wardrobe."

The great city in which he lived was always very merry; every day a number of strangers arrived there. One day two cheats came; they pretended to be weavers, and declared that they could weave the finest cloth anyone could imagine. Not only were their colors and patterns uncommonly beautiful, they said, but the clothes made of the cloth possessed the wonderful quality of becoming invisible to anyone who was unfit for his job, or was incredibly stupid.

"Those would be wonderful clothes," thought the Emperor. "If I wore those, I would be able to find out which men in my empire are not fit for the places they have. I could distinguish the clever from the stupid. Yes, this cloth must be woven for me directly!" And he gave the two cheats a great deal of money, so they might begin their work at once.

As for them, they put up two looms, and pretended to be working, but they had nothing at all on their looms. They at once demanded the finest silk and the costliest gold; this they put into their own pockets, and worked at the empty looms till late into the night.

"I should like to know how much they have done," thought the Emperor. But he felt quite uncomfortable when he thought that those who were not fit for their jobs could not see the cloth. He believed that he had nothing to fear for himself, but yet he preferred to send someone else first to see how matters stood. All the people in the whole city knew what peculiar power the stuff possessed, and all were anxious to see how bad or how stupid their neighbors were.

"I will send my honest old Minister to the weavers," thought the Emperor. "He can judge best how the stuff looks, for no one does his job better than he."

Now the good old Minister went out into the hall where the two cheats sat working at the empty looms.

"God help us!" thought the Minister, and he opened his eyes wide. "I cannot see anything at all!" But he did not say this.

Both the cheats begged him to be kind enough to come nearer, and asked if he did not approve of the colors and the pattern. Then they pointed to the empty loom, and the poor old Minister went on opening his eyes, but he could see nothing, for there was nothing to see.

"Mercy!" thought he, "can I indeed be so stupid! I never thought that, and not a soul must know it. Am I not fit for my job?— No, it will never do for me to tell that I could not see the stuff."

"Don't you have anything to say about it?" said one of the weavers.

"Oh, it is charming—quite enchanting!" answered the old Minister, as he peered through his spectacles. "What a fine pattern, and what colors! Yes, I shall tell the Emperor that I am very much pleased with it."

"Well, we are glad of that," said both the weavers, and then they named the colors, and explained the strange pattern. The old Minister listened attentively, that he might be able to repeat it when he went back to the Emperor. And he did so.

Now the cheats asked for more money, and more silk and gold, which they declared they wanted for weaving. They put it all into their own pockets, and not a thread was put upon the loom. But they continued to work at the empty frames as before.

The Emperor soon sent another honest statesman to see how the weaving was getting on. Just like the first, he looked and looked, but he could see nothing but empty looms.

"Is that not a pretty piece of cloth?" asked the two cheats, and they displayed and explained the handsome pattern which was not there at all.

"I am not stupid!" thought the man. "It must be my good job, for which I am not fit. It is strange enough, but I must not let it be noticed." And so he praised the stuff which he did not see, and expressed his pleasure at the beautiful colors and the charming pattern. "Yes, it is enchanting," he said to the Emperor.

All the people in the town were talking of the gorgeous stuff. The Emperor wished to see it himself while it was still upon the loom. With a whole crowd of chosen men, among whom were also the two men who had already been there, he went to the two cunning cheats, who were now weaving with might and main without fiber or thread.

"Is that not splendid?" said the two old men who had already been there once. "Does not your majesty notice the pattern and the colors?" And then they pointed to the empty loom, for they thought that the others could see the stuff.

"What's this?" thought the Emperor. "I can see nothing at all! That is terrible. Am I stupid? Am I not fit to be emperor? That would be the most dreadful thing that could happen to me."

"Oh, it is very pretty!" he said aloud. "It has our exalted approval." And he nodded in a contented way, and gazed at the empty loom, for he would not say that he saw nothing. The whole group of people with him looked and looked, and saw nothing, any more than the rest. But, like the Emperor, they said, "That is pretty!" and counseled him to wear these splendid new clothes for

the first time at the great procession that was soon to take place.

The Emperor was so pleased, he gave each of the cheats the title of Imperial Court Weaver.

The whole night before the morning on which the procession was to take place, the cheats were up, and had lighted more than sixteen candles. The people could see that they were hard at work, completing the Emperor's new clothes. They pretended to take the stuff down from the loom; they made cuts in the air with great scissors; they sewed with needles without thread. At last they said, "The clothes are ready."

The Emperor came with his noblest knights, and the two cheats lifted up one arm as if they were holding something and said, "See, here are the trousers! Here is the coat! Here is the cloak! It is as light as a spider's web; one would think one had nothing on, but that is just the beauty of it."

"Yes," said all the knights, but they could not see anything.

The Emperor took off his clothes, and the cheats pretended to put on him each of the new garments. As they pretended, the Emperor turned round and round before the mirror.

"Oh, how magnificent they look! How well they fit!" said all. "What a pattern! What colors! Those are splendid clothes!"

"Well, I am ready," replied the Emperor. "Does it not suit me well?" And then he turned to the mirror, for he wanted it to appear that he was studying his clothes with great interest.

The chamberlains, who were to carry the train, stooped down with their hands toward the floor, just as if they were picking up the mantle. Then they pretended to be holding something up in the air. They did not dare to let it be noticed that they saw nothing.

So the Emperor went in procession under the rich canopy, and everyone in the streets said, "The Emperor's new clothes are unlike any we have ever seen! What a train he has to his mantle! How it fits him!" No one would let it be thought that he could see nothing, for that would have shown that he was not fit for his job, or was very stupid. No clothes of the Emperor's had ever been such a success.

"But he has nothing on!" a little child cried out at last.

"Just hear what that innocent says!" said the father, and one whispered to another what the child had said. "There is a little child who says he has nothing on."

"But he has nothing on!" said the whole people at length. And the Emperor shivered, for it seemed to him that they were right. But he thought within himself, "I must go through with the procession." And so he carried himself still more proudly, and the chamberlains held on tighter than ever and carried the train which did not exist at all.

THE TRAVELING COMPANION

Kindness is always rewarded, even when it is done for those we don't know. The hero of this story gave all he had at a very sad time of his life. You will see what happened because of it. "Do not forget to entertain strangers, for by so doing some people have entertained angels without knowing it." (Hebrews 13:2)

Poor John was in great tribulation, for his father was very ill and could not get well again. The two of them were alone in the little room; the lamp on the table had nearly gone out, and it was quite late in the evening.

"You have been a good son, John," said the sick father. "God will help you through the world." And he looked at him fondly, drew a deep breath, and died. John wept; for now he had no one in the world, neither father nor mother, neither sister nor brother. Poor John!

At last his eyes closed in sleep, and he dreamed a strange dream: he saw the sun and moon curtsy to him, and he saw his father again, fresh and well, and he heard his father laugh as he had always laughed when he was very glad. A beautiful girl, with a golden crown upon her long, beautiful hair, gave him her hand, and his father said, "Do you see what a bride you have gained? She is the most beautiful in the whole world!" Then he awoke, and all the splendor was gone.

The next week the father was buried. The son walked close behind the coffin, and could now no longer see the good father who had loved him so much. Around him they were singing a psalm; it sounded so beautiful, and tears came into John's eyes. He wept, and that did him good in his sorrow. The sun shone magnificently on the green trees, just as if it were saying, "Don't be sorrowful, John! Do you see how beautifully blue the sky is? Your father is up there, and asks the Father of all that it may be always well with you."

"I will always be good and trust in God," said John, "then I shall go to heaven to my father, and what joy that will be when we see each other again! How much I shall have to tell him! And he will show me so many things, and explain to me so much of the glories of heaven, just as he taught me here on earth. Oh, how joyful that will be!"

He saw that so plainly that he smiled, while the tears were still rolling down his cheeks. The little birds sat up in the chestnut trees and twittered, "Tweet-weet! Tweet-weet!" They were joyful and merry, though they had been at the burying, for they knew quite well that the dead man was now in heaven. They knew he was now happy, because he had been a good man upon earth and had loved God, and they were glad of it. John saw how the birds flew from the green trees out into the world, and he wanted to fly too. But first he cut out a great cross of wood to put on his father's grave. And when he brought it there in the evening, the grave was decked with sand and flowers. Strangers had done this, for they were all very fond of the good father.

Early next morning, John packed his little bundle and put into his belt his whole inheritance, which consisted of fifty dollars and a few nickels. With this he intended to wander out into the world. But first he went to the churchyard, to his father's grave, repeated the Lord's Prayer, and said, "Farewell, dear father, I will always be good, and so please ask God that things may go well for me."

John turned back one more time to look at the old church, in which he had been christened when he was a little child, and where he had been every Sunday with his father at the service, and had sung his psalm. Then, high up in one of the openings of the tower, he saw a small, white bird. John nodded a farewell to him, and the little bird whistled a sweet tune to show that he wished the traveler well and hoped he would have a prosperous journey.

John thought what a number of fine things he would get to see in the great splendid world, and he traveled farther than he had ever been before. He did not know the places at all through which he came, nor the people whom he met. He was far away in a strange region.

*   *   *   *   *

The first night he had to lie under a haystack in the field to sleep, for he had no other bed. But that was very nice, he thought; the king could not be better off. There was the whole field, with the brook, the haystack, and the blue sky above it; that was certainly a beautiful sleeping room. John could sleep quite quietly, and he did so, and didn't wake until the sun rose and all the little birds were singing, "Good morning! Good morning! Are you not up yet?"

The bells were ringing for church; it was Sunday. The people went to hear the preacher, and John followed them, and sang a psalm and heard God's Word. It seemed to him just as if he were in his own church, where he had been christened and had sung psalms with his father.

That evening the weather became terribly bad. John looked for shelter, but dark night soon came on; so he went back to the little church, which lay quite solitary on a small hill.

The door luckily stood ajar, and he crept in; here he decided to remain till the storm had gone down.

"Here I will sit down in a corner," said he. "I am quite tired and require a little rest." Then he sat down, folded his hands, and said his evening prayer. Before he was aware of it he was asleep and dreaming, while it thundered and lightened outside.

When he woke it was midnight, but the bad weather had passed by, and the moon shone in upon him through the windows. In the middle of the church stood an open coffin with a dead man in it who had not yet been buried. John was not at all timid, for he had a good conscience, and he knew very well that the dead do not harm anyone. It is living people who do harm. Two such living bad men stood close by the dead man, who had been placed here in the church till he could be buried. They had an evil plot against him, and would not let him rest quietly in his coffin, but were going to throw him out before the church door—the poor dead man!

"What are you doing?" asked John. "That is wrong and wicked. Let him rest, for mercy's sake."

"Nonsense!" replied the bad men. "He has cheated us. He owed us money and could not pay it, and now he's dead and we shall not get a penny! So we will get our revenge. He shall lie like a dog outside the church door!"

"I have only fifty dollars," cried John. "That is my whole

inheritance. But I will gladly give it to you, if you will honestly promise me to leave the poor dead man in peace. I shall manage to get on without the money. I have hearty, strong limbs, and God will always help me."

"Yes," said these ugly, bad men, "if you will pay his debt we promise we will do nothing to him!" And then they took the money he gave them, laughed aloud at his good nature, and went their way. But John put the corpse back in the coffin, and folded its hands, and went away through the great forest.

*   *   *   *   *

After traveling a long way, John came out of the wood, and a strong man's voice called out behind him, "Halloo, friend! Where are you going?"

"Into the wide world!" he replied. "I have neither father nor mother, and little money, but God will help me."

"I am going out into the wide world too," said the strange man. "Shall we keep one another company?"

"Yes, certainly," said John, and so they went on together. Soon they became good friends, for they were both good souls. But John saw that the stranger was much more clever than himself. He had traveled through almost the whole world, and could tell of almost everything that existed.

*   *   *   *   *

They traveled for many, many miles over the mountains, till at last they saw a great town before them with hundreds of towers, which glittered like silver in the sun. In the midst of the town was a splendid marble palace, roofed with red gold. And there the King lived.

John and the Traveling Companion would not go into the town

at once, but remained in the inn outside the town, that they might dress themselves, for they wished to look nice when they came out into the streets. The host told them that the King was a very good man, who never did harm to anyone. But his daughter, my goodness! She was a bad princess. She possessed beauty—but of what use was that? She was a wicked girl, and because of her, many gallant princes had lost their lives. She had given permission to all men to seek her hand. Anyone might come, be he prince or beggar; it was all the same to her. He had only to guess three things about which she had thought. If he could do that, she would marry him, and he was to be king over the whole country when her father should die. But if he could not guess the three things, he would die. So evil and so wicked was the beautiful Princess.

Her father, the old King, was very sorry about it, but he could not forbid her to be so wicked, because he had once said that he would have nothing to do with her suitors; she might do as she liked. The old King was so sorry for all this misery and woe, that he used to go down on his knees with all his soldiers for a whole day in every year, praying that the Princess might become good. But she never did.

"The horrible Princess!" said John. "If I were the old King, she should be punished!"

Then they heard the people outside shouting, "Hurrah!" The Princess came by, and she was really so beautiful that all the people forgot how wicked she was. Twelve beautiful girls, all in white silk gowns, and each with a golden tulip in her hand, rode on coal-black steeds at her side. The Princess herself had a snow-white horse, decked with diamonds and rubies. Her riding clothes were made of cloth of gold, and the whip she held in her hand looked like a sunbeam. The golden crown on her head was just like little stars out of the sky, and her mantle was sewn together out of more than a thousand beautiful butterflies' wings. She herself was much more lovely than all her clothes.

When John saw her, his face became as red as a drop of blood, and he could hardly utter a word. The Princess looked just like the beautiful lady with the golden crown of whom he had dreamt on the night when his father died. He thought her so enchanting that he could not help loving her greatly. It could not be true that she was wicked, he thought.

"Everyone has permission to seek her hand, even the poorest beggar. I will go to the castle, for I cannot help doing it!"

They all told him not to attempt it, for certainly he would fare as all the others had done. His Traveling Companion, too, tried to dissuade him, but John thought it would end well. First thing the next morning, he planned to brush his shoes and his coat, wash his face and his hands, comb his beautiful hair, and then go quite alone into the town and to the palace.

*   *   *   *   *

Early the next morning, as soon as John awoke, the Traveling Companion told John he'd had a wonderful dream in the night about the Princess and her shoe. He therefore begged John to ask if the Princess had not thought about her shoe.

"I may just as well ask about that as about anything else," said John.

Then they said farewell, and John went into the town to the palace. The entire hall was filled with people; the judges sat in their armchairs and had eiderdown pillows behind their heads, for they had a great deal to think about. The old King stood up and wiped his eyes with a white pocket handkerchief. Now the

Princess came in. She was much more beautiful than yesterday, and bowed to all in a very friendly manner. But to John she gave her hand and said, "Good morning to you."

Now John had to guess what she had thought of. Oh, how lovingly she looked at him! But as soon as she heard the single word "shoe" pronounced, she became as white as chalk and trembled all over. John had guessed right!

Wonderful! How glad the old King was! He threw a somersault beautiful to behold, and all the people clapped their hands in honor of him and of John, who had guessed right the first time.

The Traveling Companion beamed with delight when he heard how well things had gone. But John folded his hands and thanked God, who certainly would help him also the second and third time. The next day he was to guess again.

The evening passed just like that of yesterday. In the morning, the Traveling Companion helped John once again. The Princess was to think of her glove, which the Traveling Companion told to John as if it had been a dream. Thus John guessed correctly, which caused great rejoicing in the palace. The whole court threw somersaults, just as they had seen the King do the first time. But the Princess lay on the sofa and would not say a single word. Now, the question was, if John could guess properly the third time. If he succeeded, he was to have the beautiful Princess and inherit the whole kingdom.

* * * * *

That evening John went early to bed, said his prayers, and went to sleep quietly. In the morning, the Traveling Companion gave John a handkerchief and told him not to untie it until the Princess asked him to tell her thoughts.

There were so many people in the great hall of the palace that they stood as close together as carrots bound together in a bundle. The council sat in the chairs with the soft pillows, and the old King wore his most stately clothes. The golden crown and scepter were polished brightly.

But the Princess was very pale. "Of what have I thought?" she asked John.

He immediately untied the handkerchief and saw inside a lovely rose. "It is a rose," he said. But the Princess sat just like a statue and could not utter a single word. At length she stood up and gave John her hand, for he had guessed correctly. She did not look at anyone, only sighed aloud, and said, "Now you will be my husband! This evening we will hold our wedding."

"I like that!" cried the old King. "This is as it should be."

All present cried, "Hurrah!" The soldiers' band played music in the streets, the bells rang, and joy now reigned everywhere. Three oxen, roasted whole and stuffed with ducks and fowls, were placed in the middle of the market, that everyone might cut himself a slice. And whoever bought a penny cake at a baker's got six buns into the bargain—and the buns had raisins in them. In the evening the whole town was lit up; the soldiers fired off the cannon, and the boys let off firecrackers. There was eating and drinking, clinking of glasses, and dancing in the palace. All the noble gentlemen and pretty ladies danced with each other, and one could hear their singing a long distance off.

* * * * *

But still the Princess was wicked and did not like John. This had been expected by the Traveling Companion, and so he gave John three petals from the rose which had been hidden in the handkerchief. He told John that he must put a large tub of water before the Princess's bed, and when the Princess was about to get into bed, he should give her a little push, so that she should fall into the tub. Then he must dip her three times, after he had put in the petals. She would then lose her evil qualities and love him very much.

John did all that the Traveling Companion had advised him to do. The Princess cried out loudly while he dipped her in the tub, but she soon changed. Her wickedness was gone. More beautiful even than before, she thanked him with tears in her lovely eyes.

The next morning the old King came with his whole court, and then there were many congratulations till late into the day. Last of all came the Traveling Companion; he had his staff in his hand and his knapsack on his back. John hugged him tightly, and said he must not depart—he must remain with the friend to whom he had brought so much happiness. But the Traveling Companion shook his head and said mildly and kindly, "Now, now, my time is up. Do you remember the dead man whom the bad people wished to harm? You gave all you possessed so that he might have a good burial. Because of that act of kindness, the Lord sent an angel to help you. For you remember that He said, 'Whatever you did for one of the least of these brothers of mine, you did for me.' "

And in the same moment the Traveling Companion sprouted a pair of beautiful white wings and flew out the window to vanish into the heavens.

The wedding festivities lasted a whole month. John and the Princess loved each other truly, and the old King passed many pleasant days, and let their little children ride on his knees and play with his scepter. And John afterwards became king over the whole country.

THE UGLY DUCKLING

*"Do not consider his appearance or his height. . . .
The LORD does not look at the things man looks at.
Man looks at the outward appearance, but the LORD looks
at the heart." (I Samuel 16:7) This is what God said when
He chose a shepherd boy to be the new king of Israel. The
Bible is full of people like the Ugly Duckling, who were
teased and laughed at because they were different, but who
grew up to be swans.*

The Mother Duck sat on her nest. "This last egg is taking a long time," she said to her visitor. "It will not burst. Now, look at the others; are they not the prettiest ducklings you have ever seen?"

"Let me see the egg which will not burst," said the Old Duck. "Believe me, it is a turkey's egg. I was once cheated in that way, and had much trouble with the young ones, for they are afraid of the water. I could not get them to venture in. I quacked and clucked, but it was no use. Let me see the egg. Yes, that's a turkey's egg! Let it lie there, and teach the other children to swim."

"I think I will sit on it a little longer," said the Duck. "I've sat so long now that I can sit a few days more."

"Just as you please," said the Old Duck, and she went away.

At last the great egg burst. "Peep! Peep!" said the little one, and crept forth. It was very large and very ugly.

"It's a very large duckling," said the Mother Duck. "None of the others look like that. Can it really be a turkey chick? We shall soon find out. It must go into the water, even if I have to kick it in myself."

The next day the weather was splendidly bright, and the sun shone all around. The Mother Duck went down to the water with all her little ones. *Splash!* She jumped into the water. "Quack! Quack!" she said, and one duckling after another plunged in. The water closed over their heads, but they came up in an instant, and swam quite well. Their legs moved by themselves, and there they were all in the water. The ugly grey Duckling swam with them.

"No, it's not a turkey," said the Mother. "Look how well it can use its legs, and how upright it holds itself. It is my own child! On the whole it's quite pretty, if one looks at it the right way. Quack!

Quack! Come with me, and I'll lead you out into the great world and present you in the poultry yard. But keep close to me, so that no one may step on you, and be careful of the cat!"

And so they came into the poultry yard. There was a terrible riot going on there, for two families were quarreling about a fish head, and the cat got it in the end.

"See, that's how it goes in this world!" said the Mother Duck. And she licked her beak, for she, too, wanted the fish head. "Now stand up straight and walk properly," she said. "And bow your heads before the Old Duck yonder. She's the grandest of all here."

They bowed, but the other ducks round about looked at them and said quite boldly, "Look there! Now we'll have these hanging on as if there were not enough of us already! And—my word!— how that Duckling yonder looks! We can't let it stay!" And one duck flew up immediately, and bit it in the neck.

"Let it alone," said the Mother. "It does no harm to anyone."

"Yes, but it's too large and peculiar," said the duck who had bitten it. "And therefore it must be beaten."

"Those are pretty children that the Mother has there," said the Old Duck with the rag round her leg. "They're all pretty but that one. That was a failure. I wish she could fix it."

"That cannot be done, my lady," replied the Mother Duck. "It is not pretty, but it has a very good heart, and swims as well as any other. I may even say it swims better. I think it will grow up pretty and become smaller in time. It stayed too long in the egg, and therefore is not properly shaped." Then she pinched it in the neck and smoothed its feathers. "Moreover, it is a drake," she said, "and therefore it is not of so much consequence. I think he will be very strong. He will turn out all right."

"The other ducklings are graceful enough," said the Old Duck. "Make yourself at home, and if you find a fish head, you may bring it to me."

And now they were at home. But the poor Duckling which had crept last out of the egg, and looked so ugly, was bitten and teased, as much by the ducks as by the chickens.

"It is too big!" they all said. And the turkey blew himself up like a ship in full sail and bore straight down upon it. Then he gobbled loudly and grew quite red in the face. The poor Duckling did not know what to do; it was quite sad because it looked ugly and was laughed at by the whole yard.

So it went on the first day, and afterwards it became worse and worse. The poor Duckling was hunted about by everyone, and so it flew away. Thus it came out into the great moor, where the wild ducks lived. Here it lay the whole night long, and it was weary and downcast.

* * * * *

Toward morning the wild ducks flew up and looked at their new companion.

"What sort of a duck are you?" they asked. The Duckling turned in every direction and bowed as well as it could. "You are remarkably ugly!" said the wild ducks. "But we don't care as long as you do not marry into our family."

Poor thing! It certainly did not think of marrying, and only hoped to lie among the reeds and drink some water.

That's how it was for two whole days; then two wild geese came by, or properly speaking, two wild ganders. It was not long since each had crept out of an egg, and that's why they were so rude.

"Listen, friend," said one of them. "You're so ugly that I like you.

Will you migrate with us and fly away from here? Near here, in another moor, there are a few sweet, lovely wild geese, all unmarried, and all able to say 'Quack!' You've a chance of making your fortune, even though you are ugly!"

Piff! Paff! resounded through the air, and the two ganders fell down dead in the swamp, and the water became blood-red. *Piff! Paff!* it sounded again, and whole flocks of wild geese rose up from the reeds. A great hunt was going on. The hunters were lying in wait all round the moor, and some were even sitting up in the branches of the trees, which spread far over the reeds. The hunting dogs came—*splash, splash!*—into the swamp, and the rushes and the reeds bent down on every side. That was a fright for the poor Duckling! It turned and put its head under its wing, but at that moment a frightful great dog stood close by the Duckling. His tongue hung far out of his mouth and his eyes gleamed horrible and ugly. He thrust out his nose close against the Duckling, showed his sharp teeth, and—*splash, splash!*—on he went, without seizing it.

"Oh, thank goodness!" sighed the Duckling. "I am so ugly that even the dog does not want to bite me!"

And so it lay quite quiet, while the shots rattled through the reeds, and gun after gun was fired. At last, late in the day, silence was restored. But the poor Duckling did not dare to rise up. It waited several hours before it looked round, and then hastened away out of the marsh as fast as it could. It ran on over field and meadow. There was such a storm raging that it was difficult to get from one place to another. Toward evening the Duckling came to a little miserable peasant's hut. This hut was so old and ruined that it did not know on which side it should fall, and that's why it remained standing. The storm whistled round the Duckling in such a way that the poor creature was obliged to sit down to resist it, and the tempest grew worse and worse. Then the Duckling noticed that one of the hinges of the door had given way, and the door hung so slanting that the Duckling could slip through the opening into the room, and it did so.

Here lived an old woman with her Tom Cat and her Hen. And the Tom Cat, whom she called Sonnie, could arch his back and purr. He could even give out sparks, but for that one had to stroke his fur the wrong way. The Hen had quite short little legs, and therefore she was called Chickabiddy-Shortshanks. She laid good eggs, and the woman loved her as her own child.

In the morning the strange Duckling was at once noticed, and the Tom Cat began to purr, and the Hen to cluck.

"What's this?" said the woman, and looked all round. But she could not see well, and therefore she thought the Duckling was a fat duck that had strayed. "This is a rare prize!" she said. "Now I shall have duck's eggs. We must try that."

And so the Duckling was admitted on trial for three weeks, but no eggs came. And the Tom Cat was master of the house, and the Hen was the lady, and they thought the world turned around them.

The Duckling thought one might have a different opinion, but the Hen would not allow it.

"Can you lay eggs?" she asked.

"No."

"Then you'll have the goodness to hold your tongue."

And the Tom Cat said, "Can you curve your back, and purr,

and give out sparks?"

"No."

"Then you cannot have any opinion of your own when sensible people are speaking."

And the Duckling sat in a corner and was very sad. Then the fresh air and the sunshine streamed in, and the Duckling was seized with such a strange longing to swim on the water, that it could not help telling the Hen of it.

"What are you thinking of?" cried the Hen. "You have nothing to do, that's why you have these thoughts. Purr or lay eggs, and they will pass over."

"I think I will go out into the wide world," said the Duckling.

"Yes, do go," replied the Hen.

And the Duckling went away. It swam on the water, and dived, but not a creature would speak to it because of its ugliness.

* * * * *

Now came the autumn. The leaves in the forest turned yellow and brown; the wind caught them so that they danced about, and up in the air it was very cold. One evening—the sun was just setting in its beauty—there came a whole flock of great handsome birds out of the bushes. The Duckling had never before seen anything so beautiful. They were dazzlingly white with long, flexible necks; they were swans. They uttered a very peculiar cry, spread forth their glorious wings, and flew away from that cold region to warmer lands, to open lakes.

And the ugly little Duckling felt quite strange as it watched them. It turned round and round in the water like a wheel, stretched out its neck toward them, and muttered such a strange loud cry it frightened itself. It did not know the name of those birds or where they were flying, but it loved them more than it had ever loved anyone. It was not at all envious of them. How could it think of wishing to possess such loveliness as they had?

And the winter grew cold, very cold! The Duckling was forced to swim about in the water to prevent the surface from freezing entirely. But every night the hole in which it swam about became smaller and smaller. It froze so hard that the icy covering cracked again, and the Duckling had to use its legs continually to prevent the hole from freezing up. At last it became exhausted and lay quite still, and thus froze fast into the ice.

Early in the morning a peasant came by, and when he saw what had happened, he took his wooden shoe, broke the ice crust to pieces, and carried the Duckling home to his wife. Then it came to itself again. The children wanted to play with it, but the Duckling thought they would harm it, and in its terror fluttered up into the milk pan, so that the milk spurted down into the room. The woman screamed and clapped her hands, at which the Duckling flew down into the butter tub, and then into the flour barrel and out again. What a sight! The woman screamed and struck at it with a poker. The children tumbled over one another in their efforts to catch the Duckling, and they laughed and screamed loudly! Luckily the door stood open, and the poor creature was able to slip out between the shrubs into the newly fallen snow. There it lay quite exhausted.

But it would be too sad a story if I were to tell all the misery and suffering which the Duckling had to endure in the hard winter. When the sun began to shine again and the larks to sing, it lay out on the swamp among the reeds. It was a beautiful spring.

Then all at once the Duckling raised its wings. They beat the air more strongly than before, and bore it strongly away. And before it well knew how all this happened, it found itself in a great garden, where the apple trees stood in blossom, where the lilac flowers smelled sweet and hung their long, green branches down to the winding canals. Oh, here it was so beautiful, such a gladness of spring! And from the thicket came three glorious white swans. They rustled their wings and swam lightly on the water.

"I will fly away to them, to the royal birds!" said the Duckling to itself. "And they will kill me, because someone so ugly would dare to approach them. Better to be killed by them than to suffer as I have!" It flew out into the water and swam toward the beautiful swans. These looked at it and came sailing down upon it with outspread wings.

"Kill me!" said the poor creature, and bent its head down upon the water, expecting nothing but death. But what was this that it saw in the clear water? It beheld its own image; and, lo! It was no longer a clumsy, dark grey bird, ugly and hateful to look at, but—a swan! And the great swans swam round it, and stroked it with their beaks.

Into the garden came little children, who threw bread and corn

into the water. The youngest cried, "There is a new one!" And the other children shouted joyously, "Yes, a new one has arrived!" And they clapped their hands and danced about, and ran to their father and mother. And bread and cake were thrown into the water, and they all said, "The new one is the most beautiful of all! So young and handsome!" And the old swans bowed their heads before it.

The young swan rustled its wings, lifted its slender neck, and cried joyfully from the depths of its heart, "I never dreamed of so much happiness when I was still the ugly Duckling!"

THE LITTLE MATCH GIRL

"He will wipe every tear from their eyes. There will be no more death or mourning or crying or pain, for the old order of things has passed away."
(Revelation 21:4)

O

utside it was terribly cold; it snowed and was already almost dark, and evening came on, the last evening of the year. In the cold and gloom a poor little girl, bareheaded and barefoot, was walking through the streets. When she left her own house she certainly had had slippers on. One slipper was lost, and a boy had seized the other and run away with it. So now the little girl walked on her little naked feet, which were quite red and blue with the cold. In an old apron she carried matches, with a bundle of them in her hand. No one had bought a thing from her all day; no one had given her a penny.

Shivering with cold and hunger she crept along, a picture of misery. The snowflakes covered her long, fair hair, which fell in pretty curls over her neck, but she did not think of that now. In all the windows lights were shining, and there was a glorious smell of roast goose, for it was New Year's Eve.

In a corner formed by two houses, one of which projected beyond the other, she sat down, shivering. She had drawn up her little feet, but she was still cold, and she did not dare to go home, for she had sold no matches and did not bring even a bit of money. Her father and mother would be displeased, and besides, it was cold at home, for they had nothing over them but a roof through which the wind whistled.

Her little hands were almost numb with the cold. Ah! A match might do her good. She drew one out. *R-r-atch!* It was a warm, bright flame, like a little candle, when she held her hands over it. It really seemed to the little girl as if she were sitting before a great polished stove, with bright brass feet and a brass cover. How comfortable it was! But the little flame went out, and the stove vanished.

A second was rubbed against the wall. It lit up, and when the light fell upon the wall it became transparent like a thin veil, and she could see through it into the room. On the table a snow-white cloth was spread; upon it stood a shining dinner service. The roast goose smoked gloriously, stuffed with apples and dried plums. Then the match went out, and only the thick, damp, cold wall was before her.

She lit another match. Then she was sitting under a beautiful Christmas tree. Thousands of candles burned upon the green branches. The girl stretched forth her hand toward them; then the match went out. She saw them now as stars in the sky; one of them fell down, forming a long line of fire.

"Now someone is dying," thought the little girl, for her old grandmother, the only person who had loved her, and who was now dead, had told her that when a star fell down, a soul went up to God.

She rubbed another match against the wall; it became bright again, and in the brightness the old grandmother stood clear and shining, mild and lovely.

"Grandmother!" cried the child. "Oh! Take me with you! I know you will go when the match is burned out. You will vanish like the warm fire, the roast goose, and the Christmas tree!"

And she rubbed the whole bundle of matches, for she wished to hold her grandmother fast. And the matches burned with such a glow that it became brighter than in the middle of the day; Grandmother had never been so large or so beautiful. She took the little girl in her arms, and both flew in brightness and joy above the earth, very, very high, and up where there was neither cold, nor hunger, nor care—they were with God!

THE
SNOW QUEEN

". . . Unless you change and become like little children, you will never enter the kingdom of heaven."
(Matthew 18:3)

I

ow we'll begin the story, and when we get to the end we shall know more than we do now.

Once upon a time there was a Troll who was the most wicked troll of them all. One day he was in very high spirits, for he had made a strange mirror that could do this: everything good and beautiful that was reflected in it shrank down to almost nothing, but anything worthless and ugly became large and looked worse than ever. The most lovely landscapes seen in this mirror looked like boiled spinach, and the best people became hideous.

The Troll wanted to fly up to heaven, to sneer and scoff at the angels themselves. Higher and higher he flew with the mirror. Suddenly it slipped out of his hands to the earth, where it was shattered into a hundred million fragments.

Now this mirror caused even more unhappiness than before; for some of the fragments were not even as large as a grain of sand. A few fragments of the mirror were so large that they were used as windowpanes, but it wasn't good to look at one's friends through these panes. Other pieces were made into glasses, and this was terrible for the people who put on these glasses to see better.

The Troll laughed till his stomach shook, for it tickled him so. But outside, some little fragments of glass still floated about in the air—and now we shall hear what happened to them.

II

In a certain large town there are so many houses and so many people that there is not enough room for everyone to have a little garden, so most people must be happy with some flowers in flowerpots. Here lived two poor children who had a garden somewhat larger than a flower pot. They were not brother and sister, but they loved each other just as much as if they had been. Their parents lived across from each other in two attics, right where the roof of one neighbor's house joined the other. Where the water pipe ran between the two houses was a little window, and one could step across the pipe to get from one window to the other.

The parents of each child had a great box, in which grew kitchen herbs that they used, and a little rosebush that grew quite well. Now it occurred to the parents to place the boxes across the pipe, so that they reached from one window to another and looked like two banks of flowers. Pea plants hung down over the boxes, and the rosebushes shot forth long twigs which clustered round the windows and bent down toward each other. It was almost like a triumphal arch of flowers and leaves. The boxes were very high, and the children knew they could not climb on them, so they often asked permission to step out on the roof behind the boxes. There they would sit on their stools under the roses and play wonderfully.

But in the winter the fun ended. The windows were sometimes quite frozen shut. But then they warmed copper coins on the stove and held the warm coins against the frozen pane. This made a great peephole, perfectly round, and behind it gleamed a pretty, mild eye at each window. These eyes belonged to the little boy and the little girl. His name was Hans and the little girl's was Gerta.

In the summer they could get to one another in one step, but in the winter they had to go down and up the long staircase, while it was snowing heavily outside.

"Those are the white bees swarming," said the old grandmother.

"Do they have a Queen Bee?" asked the little boy. For he knew that there is one among the real bees.

"Yes, they have one," replied Grandmamma. "She always flies where they swarm thickest. She is the largest of them all, and never remains quiet upon the earth. She flies up again into the black cloud. Many a midnight she is flying through the streets of the town and looks in at the windows, and then they freeze in such a strange way, and look like flowers."

"Yes, I've seen that!" cried both the children, and now they knew that it was true.

"Can the Snow Queen come in here?" asked the little girl.

"Just let her come," cried the boy. "I'll set her on the stove, and then she'll melt."

But Grandmother smoothed his hair and told more stories.

In the evening, when little Hans was at home and getting undressed, he clambered up on the chair by the window and looked through the little hole. A few flakes of snow were falling outside, and one of them, the largest of them all, was lying on the edge of one of the flower boxes. The snowflake grew larger and larger, and at last became a maiden clothed in the finest white gauze, made out of millions of starry flakes. She was beautiful and delicate, but made of ice— of shining, glittering ice. Yet she was alive; her eyes flashed like two clear stars, but there was no peace or rest in them. She nodded toward the window, and beckoned with her hand. The little boy was frightened and sprang down from the chair. Just then it seemed as if a great bird flew by outside, in front of the window.

Next day there was a clear frost, then there was a thaw, and then the spring came. The sun shone, the green leaves sprouted forth, the swallows built nests, the windows were opened, and the little children again sat in their garden high up in the roof, above all the floors.

How splendidly the roses bloomed that summer! The little girl had learned a song that talked about roses, and when she thought of her own roses, she sang this song to the little boy, and he sang too:

Our roses bloom and fade away,
Our infant Lord abides alway.
May we be blessed His face to see
And ever little children be.

The little ones held each other by the hand, kissed the roses, looked at God's bright sunshine, and spoke as if they could really see the Christ Child there. What splendid summer days those were! How beautiful it was outside, among the fresh rosebushes, which seemed as though they would never stop blooming!

Hans and Gerta sat and looked at a picture book of beasts and birds. Then, while the clock was just striking five on the church tower, Hans said, "Oh! Something struck my heart! Ouch! Something pricked me in the eye."

The little girl put her arms around his neck and looked as he blinked his eyes. No, there was nothing at all to be seen.

"I think it is gone," said he, but it was not gone. It was one of those glass fragments from the mirror. You remember the magic mirror that made everything great and good which was mirrored in it to seem small and mean, but in which the mean and the wicked things seemed larger, and every fault was noticed at once. Poor little Hans had also received a splinter just in his heart, and that would soon become like a lump of ice. It did not hurt him now, but the splinter was still there.

"Why do you cry?" he asked. "You look ugly like that. There's nothing the matter with me. Oh, look!" he suddenly exclaimed. "That rose is worm-eaten, and this one is quite crooked. They really are ugly roses. Just like the box in which they stand."

And then he kicked the box with his foot, and tore both the roses off.

"Hans, what are you doing?" cried the little girl.

And when he noticed her fright he tore off another rose, and then jumped into his own window, away from pretty little Gerta.

When she came later with her picture book, he said it was a book for babies. And when Grandmother told stories he always interrupted. When he could, he would get behind her, put on a pair of glasses, and talk just as she did. He could do that very cleverly, and people laughed, he did it so well. Soon he could mimic the speech and the walk of everybody in the street. Everything that was weird or ugly about them Hans could imitate, and people said, "That boy has a good head on his shoulders." But it was only the glass he had got in his eye, and the glass that stuck deep in his heart. He even teased little Gerta, who loved him with all her heart.

One day, Hans came by in thick gloves, with his sled on his back. He called up to Gerta, "I'm going to the great square, where the other boys play," and he was gone.

Soon the snow began to fall so thickly that the boy could not see his hand in front of him, but still he walked on. As it snowed harder, the boy became quite frightened. He wanted to say his prayers, but could remember nothing but the multiplication table.

The snowflakes became larger and larger. At last out of the snow appeared a lady, tall and slender, and brilliantly white. It was the Snow Queen.

"Why do you tremble with cold? Creep into my fur."

And she seated him beside her in her own sled and wrapped the fur round him, and he felt as if he were sinking into a snowdrift.

"Are you still cold?" asked she, and then she kissed him on the forehead.

Oh, that was colder than ice; it went quite through to his heart, half of which was already a lump of ice. He felt as if he were going to die, but only for a moment. Then he felt quite well, and he did not notice the cold all about him.

Hans looked at her. She was so beautiful, he could not imagine a more wise and lovely face. She did not appear to him to be made of ice now as before, when she sat at the window and beckoned to him. In his eyes she was perfect; he did not feel at all afraid as they flew away together.

III

But how did little Gerta feel when Hans did not return? What could have become of him? No one knew; no one could tell. Many tears were shed, and little Gerta especially wept long and bitterly. Oh, those were very dark, long winter days! But now spring came, with warmer sunshine.

"Hans is gone," said little Gerta.

"I don't believe it," said the Sunshine.

"He is gone," she said to the Swallows.

"We don't believe it," they replied, and at last little Gerta did not believe it herself.

"I will put on my new red shoes," she said one morning, "those that Hans has never seen, and then I will go down to the river and ask for him."

It was still very early. She kissed the old grandmother, who was still asleep, put on her red shoes, and went quite alone out of the town gate toward the river.

"Is it true that you have taken away my friend from me? I will give you my red shoes if you will give him back to me!"

And it seemed to her as if the waves were nodding quite strangely. So she took her red shoes, that she liked best of anything she possessed, and threw them both into the river. But they fell close to the shore, and the little waves carried them back to her. It seemed as if the river would not take from her the dearest things she possessed because it did not have her little Hans. But she thought she had not thrown the shoes far enough out, so she crept into a boat that lay among the reeds, went to the other end of the boat, and threw the shoes from there into the water. But the boat was not bound fast, and at the movement she made it glided away from the shore. She noticed it and hurried to get back, but before she reached the other end the boat was a yard from the bank, and it drifted away faster than before.

Then little Gerta was very much frightened and began to cry. But no one heard her except the Sparrows, and they could not carry her to land. They flew along by the shore and sang, as if to console her, "Here we are! Here we are!"

The boat drifted on with the stream, and little Gerta sat quite still, with only her stockings on her feet. Her little red shoes floated along behind her, but they could not catch up to the boat, for it went too fast. It was very pretty on both shores. There were beautiful flowers, old trees, and slopes with sheep and cows, but not one person was to be seen.

"Perhaps the river will carry me to little Hans," thought Gerta.

At that thought she became more cheerful. For many hours she watched the charming green banks; then she came to a great cherry orchard, in which stood a little house with remarkable blue and red windows. It had a thatched roof, and two wooden soldiers stood outside, who presented arms to those who sailed past.

Gerta called to them, for she thought they were alive, but of course they did not answer. She came quite close to them as the river carried the boat toward the shore.

Gerta called still louder, and then there appeared a beautiful garden. She drew the boat to land and searched among the flower beds, but found no one.

She sat down and wept, her tears falling upon a spot where a rosebush lay buried. As the warm tears touched the earth, the bush at once sprouted up. Gerta kissed the Roses and thought of the beautiful roses at home, and also of little Hans.

"Do you know where Hans is?" she asked the Roses. "Do you think he is dead?"

"He is not dead," the Roses answered.

"Thank you," said little Gerta. And she went to the other flowers, looked into their cups, and asked, "Do you not know where little Hans is?"

But every flower stood in the sun thinking only of her own story or fairy tale. Gerta listened to many of their stories, but not one knew anything of Hans.

So she ran to the end of the garden. At last she could run no longer, and seated herself on a great stone. When she looked round, the summer was over—it was late in autumn. One did not notice that in the beautiful garden, because there was always sunshine, and the flowers of every season always bloomed.

"Oh dear! I've wasted so much time!" said little Gerta. "It's already autumn. I cannot rest again."

And she rose up to go on. Oh! How sore and tired her little feet were. All around it looked cold and bleak. The long willow leaves were quite yellow, and the mist dropped from them like water; one leaf after another dropped. Only the sloe-thorn still bore fruit, but the sloes were sour, and set the teeth on edge. Oh! How grey and gloomy the whole, wide world looked!

IV

Gerta had to rest again. Just then a crow landed in the snow, just opposite the spot where she was sitting. This Crow had sat looking at her a long time, nodding its head. Then it said, "Caw! Caw! Good day! Good day!" It could not talk very well, but it felt friendly toward the little girl and asked where she was going all alone in the wide world. The word "alone" Gerta understood very well, and she felt very alone just then. She told the Crow the whole story of her life, and asked if it had not seen Hans.

The Crow nodded very gravely and said, "That may be! That may be!"

"What, do you think so?" cried the little girl, and nearly hugged the Crow to death, she kissed it so.

"Gently, gently!" said the Crow. "I think I know. I believe it might be little Hans, but he has certainly forgotten you, with the Prince and Princess."

"Does he live with a Prince and Princess?" asked Gerta.

"Yes, but I must tell you," said the Crow, "a little girl like your-self will never be allowed to go in."

"Yes, I shall be allowed," said Gerta. "When Hans hears that I'm here, he'll come out directly and bring me in."

They went into the garden, into the great avenue, where one leaf was falling down after another. When the lights went out in the palace, one after the other, the Crow led Gerta to a back door, which stood open.

Oh, how Gerta's heart beat with fear and longing! She felt just like she was going to do something wrong, and yet she only wanted to know if she had found Hans. Yes, it must be him. She thought of his clear eyes and his long hair. She thought she could see him smile as he had smiled at home when they sat among the roses. He would certainly be glad to see her, to hear what a long distance she had come for his sake, and to know how sorry they had all been at home when he did not come back. She was so afraid and so glad at the same time!

Now they came into the first hall. It was hung with rose-col-ored satin, and artificial flowers were worked on the walls. Here the dreams came flitting by them, but they moved so quickly that Gerta could not see the noble lords and ladies. Each hall was more splendid than the last, so that one almost became confused about which room one was in! At last they came to the bedchamber. Here the ceiling was like a great palm tree with leaves of costly glass, and in the middle of the floor two beds hung on a thick stalk of gold, and each of them looked like a lily. One of them was white, and in that lay the Princess. The other was red, and in that Gerta was to find little Hans. She bent one of the red leaves aside, and then she saw a little brown neck. Oh, that was Hans! She called out his name quite loudly and held the lamp toward him. The dreams rushed into the room again on horseback—he awoke, turned his head, and—it was not little Hans!

The Prince was only like him in the neck, but he was young and good-looking. The Princess looked up, blinking, from the white lily, and asked who was there. Then little Gerta wept and told her whole story, and all that the Crow had done for her.

"You poor child!" said the Prince and Princess.

The Prince got up out of his bed and let Gerta sleep in it, and he could not have done anything better. She folded her little hands and thought, "How good both men and animals are!" And then she shut her eyes and went quietly to sleep. All the dreams came flying in again, looking like angels, and they drew a little sled, on which Hans sat nodding. But all this was only a dream, and therefore it was gone again as soon as she awoke.

The next day she was clothed from head to foot in silk and velvet. And she was told she could stay in the castle and enjoy pleasant times. But she only begged for a little carriage, with a horse to draw it, and a pair of little boots. Then she would drive out into the world and look for Hans.

She received not only boots, but a muff, too, and was neatly dressed. When she was ready to depart, a coach made of pure gold stopped before the door. Upon it the coat of arms of the Prince and Princess shone like a star. A coachman, footmen, and two other servants sat on horseback with gold crowns on their heads. The Prince and Princess themselves helped her into the carriage and wished her all good fortune. The coach was lined with sugar biscuits, and in the seat there were gingerbread nuts and fruit.

"Farewell, farewell!" cried the Prince and Princess.

V

They drove on through the thick forest, but the coach gleamed like a torch, and dazzled some robbers' eyes, so that they had to have it.

"That is gold! That is gold!" they cried, and they rushed forward and seized the horses. They tied up the servants, the coachman, and the footmen, and then pulled little Gerta out of the carriage.

"She is fat—she is pretty—she has been fed with nuts!" said the old robber woman, who had a very long, stiff beard and shaggy eyebrows that hung down over her eyes. "She's as good as a little pet lamb."

"Oh!" screamed the old woman, for just then her own daughter, who hung at her back, bit her ear in a very naughty and spiteful manner.

"She shall play with me!" said the little Robber Girl. "She shall give me all her pretty things!"

And then, just to make sure, the girl gave another bite, so that the woman jumped high up and turned round, and all the robbers laughed and said, "Look how she dances with the little brat."

"I want to ride in the carriage," said the little Robber Girl.

And she did, for she was spoiled and very stubborn. She and Gerta sat in the carriage and drove over old and worn paths deep into the forest. The little Robber Girl was as big as Gerta, but much stronger. She had brown skin and very black eyes that looked quite sad. She clasped little Gerta round the waist and said, "I suppose you are a princess?"

"No," replied Gerta. And she told all that had happened to her and how much she loved little Hans.

The Robber Girl looked at her seriously, nodded slightly, and said, "They shall not hurt you even if I do get angry with you, for then I will do it myself."

And then she dried Gerta's eyes, and put her two hands into the beautiful muff that was so soft and warm.

Now the coach stopped, and they were in the courtyard of a robber castle. The walls had cracked from the top to the bottom. Ravens and crows flew out of the great holes, and big bulldogs— each of which looked as if he could devour a man—jumped high up, but they did not bark, for that was forbidden.

In the great old smoky hall a bright fire burned upon the stone floor. The smoke passed along under the ceiling, looking for a way out. A great cauldron of soup was boiling and hares and rabbits were roasting over the fire.

"Tonight you shall sleep with me and all my little animals," said the Robber Girl.

They got something to eat and drink, and then went to a corner where straw and carpets were spread out. Above these, on perches, sat more than a hundred pigeons, that all seemed asleep, but they turned a little when the two little girls came in.

"All these belong to me," said the little Robber Girl. She quickly seized one of the nearest, held it by the feet, and shook it so that it flapped its wings. "Kiss it!" she cried, and held it in Gerta's face. "There sit the Wood Pigeons," she continued, pointing to some pieces of wood that had been nailed in front of a hole in the wall. "Those are wood rascals, those two. They would fly away if we did not keep them well locked up. And here's my old sweetheart, Ba."

And she pulled on the horns of a Reindeer, that was tied up and had a polished copper ring round its neck. "We have to keep him tied tight too, or he'd run away from us. But now tell me again the story about little Hans, and why you came out into the wide world."

And Gerta told it again from the beginning, and the Wood Pigeons cooed above them in their cage, and the other pigeons slept. The little Robber Girl put her arm round Gerta's neck and slept soundly.

But Gerta could not close her eyes at all as the robbers sat round the fire, singing and drinking.

Then the Wood Pigeons said, "Coo! Coo! We have seen little Hans. A white hen was carrying his sled. He sat in the Snow Queen's sled, which flew low over the forest as we lay in our nests. She breathed on the young pigeons, and all died except us two. Coo! Coo!"

"What are you saying?" asked Gerta. "Where was the Snow Queen traveling? Do you know anything about it?"

"She was probably journeying to Finland, for there they always have ice and snow. Ask the Reindeer that is tied up with the cord."

"Yes, there is ice and snow there, and it is glorious," said the Reindeer. "There one can run about freely on great glittering plains. There the Snow Queen has her summer tent, but her castle is toward the North Pole, on an island called Spitzbergen."

"Oh, Hans, little Hans!" cried Gerta.

"You must lie still," exclaimed the Robber Girl.

In the morning Gerta told her all that the Wood Pigeons had said. The Robber Girl looked quite serious, and nodded her head, and said, "I'm sure it's true. I'm sure it is."

"Do you know where Finland is?" she asked the Reindeer.

"Who would know better than I?" the creature replied, and its eyes sparkled. "I was born there and ran about in the snowfields."

"Listen!" said the Robber Girl to Gerta. "You see all our men have gone away. Only Mother is here still, and she'll stay. But toward noon she sleeps for a little while. Then I'll do something for you."

When the mother had gone to sleep, the Robber Girl went to

the Reindeer and said, "I'll loosen your cord and help you out, so that you may run to Finland. But you must run fast and carry this little girl to the palace of the Snow Queen, where her friend is. You've heard what she told me, for she spoke loud enough, and you were listening."

The Reindeer leaped for joy, and the Robber Girl lifted little Gerta on its back. She also thought to tie her fast, and even to give her a little cushion as a saddle.

"There are your fur boots," she said, "for it's growing cold. But I shall keep the muff, for it's so very pretty. Still, you will not be cold, for here are my mother's big mittens—they'll just reach up to your elbows. Now your hands look just as clumsy as my mother's."

And Gerta wept for joy.

"I can't bear to see you cry," said the little Robber Girl. "No, you ought to look very glad. And here are two loaves and a ham for you, so you won't be hungry."

These were tied on the Reindeer's back. The little Robber Girl opened the door, brought in all the big dogs, and then cut the rope and said to the Reindeer, "Now run, but take good care of the little girl."

And Gerta waved her hands with the big mittens toward the little Robber Girl and said, "Good-bye!"

The Reindeer ran away through the great forest, over marshes and plains, as fast as it could go. The wolves howled and the ravens croaked. Something in the air went, "Hiss! hiss!" And suddenly it seemed as if the sky were flashing fire.

"Those are the Northern Lights," said the Reindeer. "Look how they glow!" And then it ran on faster than ever, day and night.

The loaves were eaten, and the ham as well, and at last they were in Finland.

VI

When they got to Finland, they knocked at the chimney of a hut, for they could not find the door.

It was so hot inside the house that the woman in it went about with almost nothing on. She was little and very dirty. She at once loosened little Gerta's dress and took off the child's mittens and boots, otherwise it would have been too hot for her to bear. Then she laid a piece of ice on the Reindeer's head and asked why the two travelers had come to her home.

Now the Reindeer first told his own story, and then little Gerta's, and the Finland Woman blinked with her clever eyes but said nothing.

"You are very clever," said the Reindeer. "I know you can tie all the winds of the world together in four knots on a bit of twine. If the sailor unties one knot, he has a good wind; if he loosens the second, it blows hard, but if he unties the third and the fourth, such a storm comes up that the forests are thrown down. Won't you give the little girl a potion that will give her the strength of twelve men, so she can overcome the Snow Queen?"

"The strength of twelve men!" repeated the Finland Woman. "A lot of use that would be!" She went to a shelf, and brought out a great rolled-up fur and unrolled it. Wonderful characters were written upon it, and the Finland Woman read until sweat ran down her forehead.

The Reindeer again begged so hard for little Gerta, and Gerta looked at the Finland Woman with her eyes full of tears, until finally the Finland Woman blinked, and drew the Reindeer into a corner, and whispered to him, as she laid fresh ice upon his head.

"Little Hans is certainly at the Snow Queen's, and he likes everything there so much that he thinks it is the best place in the world. But that is because he has a splinter of glass in his eye, and a little fragment in his heart. These must be taken out, or he will never be a human being again, and the Snow Queen will keep her power over him."

"But cannot you give something to little Gerta, to give her power over all this?"

"I can give her no greater power than she possesses already. Don't you see how great that is? Don't you see how men and animals serve her, and how she came this far in her bare feet? Her power lies in her heart; her power is that she is a dear innocent child. If she herself cannot get to the Snow Queen and get the glass out of little Hans, then we have no hope of doing it! Two miles from here the Snow Queen's garden begins; you can carry the little girl there. Set her down by the great bush that stands with its red berries in the snow. Don't stand talking, but hurry, and get back here!"

Then the Finland Woman lifted little Gerta onto the Reindeer, which ran as fast as it could.

"Oh, I forgot my boots! I forgot my mittens!" cried Gerta.

She soon felt the cold cutting through to her bones, but the

Reindeer dared not stop. It ran till it came to the bush with the red berries, and there it set Gerta down. It kissed her, and great bright tears ran over the creature's cheeks. Then it ran back, as fast as it could. There stood poor Gerta without shoes, without mittens, in the midst of terrible, cold Finland.

She ran forward as fast as she could. Then a whole regiment of snowflakes came toward her, but they did not fall down from the sky. The snowflakes ran along the ground, and the nearer they came, the larger they grew. Gerta still remembered how large and beautiful the snowflakes had appeared when she looked at them through the magnifying glass. But here they were certainly far larger and much more terrible—they were alive. They were the guards of the Snow Queen, and had the strangest shapes. A few looked like ugly, great porcupines; others like knots of snakes. Still others looked like little fat bears, whose hair stood on end. All were brilliantly white, and all were living snowflakes.

Then little Gerta said a prayer, and the cold was so great that she could see her own breath, which went forth out of her mouth like smoke. The breath formed itself into little angels, who grew and grew whenever they touched the earth. They all had helmets on their heads and shields and spears in their hands. Their number increased more and more, and when Gerta had finished her prayer, a whole army of angels stood around her. They struck with their spears at the terrible snowflakes, so that they were shattered into a thousand pieces, and little Gerta went by unharmed and full of courage. The angels stroked her hands and feet, and then she didn't feel so cold, and went on to the Snow Queen's palace.

But now we must see what Hans is doing. He was not thinking of little Gerta, and never would have thought that she was standing right in front of the palace.

VII

The walls of the palace were formed of the drifting snow, and the windows and doors of the cutting winds. There were more than a hundred halls, all blown together by the snow. The greatest of these extended for several miles, and the strong Northern Lights lit them all. Empty, vast, and cold were the halls of the Snow Queen. In the midst of this immense, empty, snow hall was a frozen lake, which had burst into a thousand pieces. But each piece was like the rest, so that it was a perfect work of art. And in the middle of the lake sat the Snow Queen when she was at home. And she called the lake the Mirror of Reason, and said it was the only one, and the best in the world.

Little Hans was quite blue with cold—but he did not notice it, for she had kissed the cold shudderings away from him, and his heart was now like a lump of ice. He dragged a few sharp flat pieces of ice to and fro, joining them together, trying to make something out of them. Hans laid the ice in designs and patterns, and, indeed, very artistic ones. He called it the Game of Reason. In his eyes these figures were very remarkable and of the highest importance; that was because of the fragment of glass sticking in his eye. He tried to lay out the figures so that they formed a word—but he could never manage to lay down the word he wanted—the word "Eternity." The Snow Queen had said, "If you can figure this out, you shall be your own master, and I will give you the whole world and a new pair of skates."

But he could not.

"Now I'm going away to the warm lands," said the Snow Queen. "I will go and look into the black pots." Those were the volcanoes, Etna and Vesuvius. "I will touch them with ice. That will be just what they need."

The Snow Queen flew away, and Hans sat quite alone in the great icy hall that was miles long. He looked at his pieces of ice and thought so hard that cracks were heard inside him. He sat so stiff and still, he appeared frozen to death.

Then little Gerta stepped through the great gate into the wide hall. Here the cutting winds blew against her, but she prayed a prayer, and they lay down as if they had gone to sleep. She stepped into the great, empty, cold halls, and there she saw Hans. She knew him at once, and flew to him and hugged him, and held him fast, and called out, "Hans, dear little Hans! At last I have found you!"

He sat quite still, stiff and cold. Little Gerta wept hot tears that fell upon his breast. They got into his heart and thawed the lump of ice and consumed the little piece of glass in it. He looked at her, and she sang:

> Our roses bloom and fade away,
> Our infant Lord abides alway.
> May we be blessed His face to see
> And ever little children be.

Then Hans burst into tears. He wept so that the splinter of glass was washed out of his eye. Now he recognized his friend and cried joyfully, "Gerta, dear Gerta! Where have you been all this time? And where have I been?" He looked all around him. "How cold it is here! How large and empty!"

And he clung to Gerta, and she laughed and wept for joy. It was so glorious that even the pieces of ice around them danced for joy. And when they were tired and lay down, they formed themselves into the letters of the word "Eternity." So now Hans could be his own master, and the Snow Queen would have to give him the whole world and a new pair of skates.

Gerta kissed Hans's cheeks, and they became rosy again. She

kissed his eyes, and they shone like her own. She kissed his hands and feet, and he became happy and healthy once more. The Snow Queen could come now; Hans's letter of freedom stood written on the lake in bright, shining letters of ice.

And they took one another by the hand and wandered out of the great palace of ice. They spoke of Grandmother, and of the roses on the roof, and everywhere they went the winds stopped and the sun burst forth. When they came to the bush with the red berries, the Reindeer was standing there waiting. It had brought another young Reindeer, and the two carried Hans and Gerta to the outskirts of the town where Grandmother lived. There they said goodbye.

Gerta and Hans went hand in hand. It had become beautiful spring, with green leaves and wildflowers. The church bells sounded, and they saw the high steeples and buildings of their hometown. They went to Grandmother's door, and up the stairs, and into the room, where everything was in its usual place. The clock was ticking and the hands were turning.

But as they went through the rooms they noticed that they had become grown-up people. The roses out on the roof gutter were blooming in at the open window, and there stood the little children's chairs. Hans and Gerta sat each upon their own, and held each other by the hand. They forgot the cold, empty splendor of the Snow Queen's palace like a heavy dream. Grandmother sat in God's bright sunshine, and read aloud out of the Bible, "Unless you change and become like little children, you will never enter the kingdom of heaven."

And Hans and Gerta looked into each other's eyes, and all at once they understood the old hymn—

Our roses bloom and fade away,
Our infant Lord abides alway.
May we be blessed His face to see
And ever little children be.

There they both sat, grown-up, and yet children in heart, and it was summer, warm, delightful summer.

THE PRINCESS AND THE PEA

*You can't always tell what someone is
like just by looking at her. You never know
if somebody dressed in rags might
be a princess.*

here was once a Prince who wanted to marry a princess, but she had to be a real princess. So he traveled all through the world to find a real one, but everywhere there was something in the way. There were many princesses, but he could not tell if they were real princesses; there was always something that did not seem quite right. So he came home again, and was quite sad for he wished so much to have a real princess.

One evening a terrible storm came on. The lightning flashed, the thunder crashed, and the rain streamed down; it was quite fearful! Then there was a knocking at the town gate, and the old King went out to open it.

A princess stood outside the gate. But, mercy! how she looked, from the rain and the rough weather! The water ran down her hair and her clothes; it ran in at the points of her shoes and out at the heels. Yet she declared that she was a real princess.

"Yes, we will soon find out," thought the old Queen. But she said nothing, only went into the guest room, took all the bedding off the bed, and put a pea on the bottom of the bedstead. Then she took twenty mattresses and laid them upon the pea, and then twenty eiderdown quilts upon the mattresses. On this the Princess had to lie all night. In the morning she was asked how she had slept.

"Oh, miserably!" said the Princess. "I scarcely closed my eyes all night long. Goodness knows what was in my bed. I lay upon something hard, so that I am black and blue all over. It is quite dreadful!"

Now they saw that she was a real princess, for through the twenty mattresses and the twenty eiderdown quilts she had felt the pea. No one but a real princess could be so tender-skinned.

So the Prince took her for his wife, for now he knew that he had a true princess.

And, remember, this is a true story!

THE GIRL WHO STEPPED ON HER BREAD

"And why do you worry about clothes?" Jesus said, "Look at the flowers in the field. . . . Even Solomon with his riches was not dressed as beautifully as one of these flowers. . . . So you can be even more sure that God will clothe you." (Matthew 6:28-30, ICB). Worrying about what we look like or what we wear is a kind of pride. In this story Inger finds out that this kind of pride is a very dangerous thing—it can even give you a certain "sinking feeling."

**I**nger was a poor child, who was also proud and vain. She had a bad temper. And as she grew older she became worse instead of better. But she was very beautiful, and that was too bad. For if she had not been so pretty, she would have been punished.

"You will bring evil on your own head," said her mother. "As a little child you used to tear my aprons; when you are older you will break my heart."

And she did so sure enough.

At length she went into the country to work for people of nobility. They were as kind to her as if she were one of their own family, and she was so well-dressed that she looked very pretty and became extremely arrogant.

When she had worked for them a year, her employers said to her, "You should go and visit your family, little Inger."

She went, because she wanted them to see how fine she had become. However, when she reached the village and saw the boys and girls talking together near the pond, and her mother sitting close by on a stone resting her head against a bundle of firewood which she had picked up in the forest, Inger turned back. She felt ashamed that she, who was dressed so nicely, should have a mother who was such a ragged woman, one who gathered sticks for her fire. She didn't care that they were expecting her. She was so angry she went back to the nobles' house.

Half a year more passed.

"You must go home someday and see your old parents, little Inger," said the mistress of the house. "Here is a large loaf of white bread—you can carry this to them; they will be happy to see you."

And Inger put on her best clothes and her nice new shoes, and she lifted her dress high, and walked so carefully, that she might not dirty her garments or her feet. There was no harm at all in that. But when she came to where the path went over some damp, marshy ground, and water and mud were in the way, she threw the bread into the mud in order to step on it and get over with dry shoes. But just as she had placed one foot on the bread and had lifted the other up, the bread sank in with her deeper and deeper till she went entirely down, and nothing was to be seen but a black, bubbling pool.

*   *   *   *   *

What happened to the girl? She went below to the Moor Woman who lives below the earth. Inger sank into her home, and no one could hold out very long there. Every bottle and pot smells horrible, which would make any human being faint, and they are packed closely together and over one another. Even if there were a small space among them which one might creep through, it would be impossible, because of all the slimy toads and snakes that are always crawling and forcing themselves through.

Into this place little Inger sank. All this mess was so ice-cold that she shivered in every limb. Yes, she became stiffer and stiffer. The bread stuck fast to her, and it drew her as a needle draws a slender thread.

The Moor Woman was at home. She saw Inger, put on her spectacles, and looked at her.

"That is a girl with talents," said she. "She may do very well as a statue to ornament my great-grandchildren's bedroom." And she took her.

It was thus that little Inger was taken to another room and made a prisoner. Inger thought it shocking to stand there like a statue; she was, as it were, fastened to the ground by the bread.

"This is what comes of wishing to have clean shoes," said she to herself. "At least I have a pretty face and am well-dressed," and she dried her eyes. She was still very proud. She had not noticed how her fine clothes had been soiled in the house of the Moor Woman. Her dress was covered with dirt.

But the worst of all was the dreadful hunger she felt. Could she stoop down and break off a piece of the bread on which she was standing? No; her back was stiffened; her hands and arms were stiffened; her whole body was like a statue of stone. She could only move her eyes, and these she could turn entirely around. "If this goes on I cannot hold out much longer," she said.

But she had to hold out, and her sufferings became greater.

* * * * *

Then a warm tear fell on her head. It trickled over her face and her neck, all the way down to the bread. Another tear fell, then many followed. Who was weeping over little Inger? Her mother was crying over her up on the earth. The tears which a mother sheds over her child always reach it, but they do not comfort the bad child—they burn; they increase the suffering. And oh! this intolerable hunger; yet she couldn't snatch one mouthful of the bread under her feet! She became as thin as a reed.

Another trial was that she heard all that was said of her above on the earth, and it was nothing but blame and evil. Though her mother wept, she still said, "Pride goes before a fall. That was your great fault, Inger. Oh, how sad you have made your mother!"

Her mother and all who knew her were well aware of the sin she had committed.

She heard how the noble family who had been so kind to her

spoke. "She was a wicked child," they said. "She did not value the gifts of our Lord, but trampled them under her feet."

"They ought to have taught me better," thought Inger. "They should have driven the bad thoughts out of me, if I had any."

She heard that there was a song made about her, "The bad girl who stepped on her bread to keep her shoes clean," and this song was sung from one end of the country to the other.

"No one should have to suffer so much for what I did—be punished so much for such a little thing!" thought Inger. "Others are punished justly, for no doubt there is a great deal to punish, but ah, how I suffer!"

And her heart became even harder than the stone she had become.

"No one can be better in such a place. I will not grow better here. See how dank and dreary it is."

And her heart became still harder, and she hated everyone.

She listened and heard them telling her story as a warning to children, and the little ones called her "bad Inger." "She was so naughty," they said, "so very wicked, that she deserved to suffer."

The children always said mean things about her. One day, however, she was very hungry and sad, and she heard her story told to an innocent child—a little girl. The child burst into tears for the proud, finely dressed Inger.

"But will she never come home again?" asked the child.

The answer was: "She will never come home again."

"But if she will say she is sorry and promise never to be naughty again?"

"But she will not say she is sorry," they said.

"Oh, how I wish she would do it!" sobbed the little girl, greatly upset. "I will give my doll, and my doll's house, too, if she may come home!" These words touched Inger's heart; they almost made her good. It was the first time anyone had said "poor Inger" and had not talked about her faults. An innocent child cried and prayed for her. She was so much affected by this that she wanted to weep herself, but she could not, and this was even worse.

* * * * *

Time passed on and on, slowly and wretchedly. Then once more Inger heard her name mentioned, and she saw directly above her, two clear stars shining. These were two mild eyes that were closing up on earth. The little girl who had cried in childish sorrow over "poor Inger" was dying, and our Lord was now about to call her to Himself. Just then, she remembered how she had wept bitterly on hearing the story of Inger. She remembered that time and those feelings so well that, in the hour of death, she cried with intense emotion, "Dear God, like Inger, I have not been thankful for Your blessed gifts. I have often been guilty of pride and vanity in my secret heart. But You still loved me. Oh, do not forsake me in my last hour!"

And the little

girl's eyes closed, and her spirit's eyes opened and saw invisible things. And as she had been thinking about Inger in her latest thoughts, she saw her and how deep she had been dragged downward. At that sight she burst into tears, and in the kingdom of heaven she stood and wept because of Inger.

Her tears and her prayers sounded like an echo down in Inger's hollow, imprisoned soul. That soul was overwhelmed with the love from this child she never knew. One of God's children wept for her! Why would anyone do that for her? Inger's spirit gathered together all the bad things that it had done, and it shook with the sorrow—sorrow such as Inger had never felt. She thought that for her the gates of mercy would never open, and she would never escape.

And just as she was thinking how sorry she was, a ray of brightness penetrated into that horrid place—a ray more glorious than the sunbeams which thaw the snow. And this ray, more quickly than a snowflake melts on your tongue, caused Inger's stiff body to melt into flesh again and to fly up toward the outside world.

For a long time she sat quietly and looked out at the beauty all around. The air was so fresh, yet so soft; the moon shone so clearly; the trees and the flowers scented so sweetly, and it was so comfortable where she sat—her clothes so clean and nice. How all creation told of love and glory! The grateful thoughts that awoke in her breast she poured forth in a hymn of joy as she ran home to her mother.

THE APPLE TREE BRANCH AND THE DANDELION

Hans Christian Andersen was sometimes looked down on by his rich friends because he came from a poor family. In this story he tells his friends that any differences between people only make them more uniquely beautiful. Paul said something similar in Romans 10:12: "For there is no difference between Jew and Gentile—the same Lord is Lord of all and richly blesses all who call on him."

In a little apple tree, one branch hung fresh and blooming, covered with delicate pink blossoms that were just ready to open. The Apple Tree Branch knew well enough how beautiful he was, and was not surprised when a nobleman's carriage stopped beside him on the road. The young Countess said the Apple Branch was the loveliest thing one could behold, a very emblem of spring in its most charming form. The Branch was broken off, and she sheltered it with her silk parasol.

Then they drove to the castle, where pure white curtains fluttered round the open windows, and beautiful flowers stood in shining vases. In one of these, the Apple Branch was placed among some fresh light twigs of beech. It was charming to behold. But the Branch became proud, just like humans do.

People of various kinds came through the room, and according to their rank they might express their admiration. A few said nothing at all, and others said too much, and the Apple Branch soon understood that there was a difference in human beings just as among plants. "Some are created for beauty, and some for use, and there are some which one can do without altogether," thought the Apple Branch.

As he stood just in front of the open window, he could see into the garden and across the fields. He had flowers and plants enough to think about, for there were rich plants and humble plants— some very humble indeed.

"Poor despised herbs!" said the Apple Branch. "There is certainly a difference! How unhappy they must feel, if indeed that kind *can* feel like myself and my equals."

And the Apple Branch looked down with pity, especially upon

the dandelion. No one bound them into a nosegay, they were too common. They might be found even among the cobblestones, shooting up everywhere like weeds, and they had the ugly name of "dandelion," or "the devil's milk pail."

"Poor despised plants!" said the Apple Branch. "It is not your fault that you are what you are, that you are so common, and that you received the ugly name you bear. But it is with plants as with men—there must be a difference!"

"A difference?" said the Sunbeam, and he kissed the blooming Apple Branch, but also kissed the yellow dandelions out in the field—the poor flowers as well as the rich.

Now the Apple Branch had never thought of God's boundless love toward everything that lives and moves and has its being. He had never thought how many things that are beautiful and good may be hidden, but not forgotten.

The Sunbeam knew better and said, "You don't see far and you don't see clearly. Which plant do you especially pity?"

"The dandelion," replied the Apple Branch. "It is trodden underfoot. There are too many of them, and when they run to seed, they fly away like little pieces of wool over the roads and cling to people's clothes. They are nothing but weeds—but it is right there should be weeds, too. I'm just thankful that I am not one of those flowers."

But there came across the fields a whole troop of children. And when the smallest one was set down in the grass among the yellow flowers, it laughed aloud with glee. The elder children broke off the flowers and bent the stalks round into one another, link by link, so that a whole chain was made. They made first a necklace and then a scarf to hang over their shoulders and tie round their waists, and then a crown to wear on their heads. It was quite a gala of green links and chains.

"Do you see?" said the Sunbeam. "Do you see the beauty of those flowers? Do you see their power?"

"Yes—over children," replied the Apple Branch. "But there is a difference among plants, just as there is a difference among men."

And then the Sunbeam spoke of the boundless love of the Creator, as shown in the creation, and of the perfect balance of things in time and in eternity.

"Yes, yes, that is your opinion," the Apple Branch persisted.

But now some people came into the room with the beautiful young Countess, the lady who had placed the Apple Branch in the vase in the sunlight. She carried something in her hand. The object, whatever it might be, was hidden by three or four great leaves wrapped around it like a shield. It was carried more carefully than the Apple Branch had been. Very gently the large leaves were now removed, and lo, there appeared the fine feathery seed crown of the despised dandelion!

"Look at the beauty God has given it," she said. "I will paint it, together with the Apple Tree Branch, whose beauty all have admired. But this humble flower has received just as much from God in a different way, and, different as they are, both are children of the kingdom of beauty."

And the Sunbeam kissed the humble flower, and he kissed the blooming Apple Branch, whose leaves appeared to blush.

THUMBELINA

No matter what our size, we must always remember what really matters in the eyes of God and other people: our patience, kindness, and love. With these three practices, even someone an inch tall can do great and mighty things.

There was once a woman who wished for a very little child, but she did not know where she could get one. So she went to an old wise woman, and said, "I do so very much wish for a little child! Can you tell me where I can get one?"

"Oh, that could easily be managed," said the wise woman. "Here is a barleycorn; it is not of the kind which grows in the countryman's field, and which the chickens get to eat. Put it into a flowerpot, and you shall see what you shall see."

"Thank you," said the woman, and she gave the old woman twelve pennies.

Then she went home and planted the barleycorn, and immediately a great handsome flower grew up, which looked like a tulip. But the leaves were tightly closed, as though it were still a bud.

"It is a beautiful flower," said the woman, and she kissed its beautiful yellow and red leaves. But just as she kissed it, the flower opened with a loud crack. It was a real tulip, as one could now see, but in the middle of the flower there sat a little maiden, delicate and graceful to behold. She was scarcely half a thumb's length in height, and therefore she was called Thumbelina.

A neat, polished walnut shell served Thumbelina for a cradle; blue violet leaves were her mattresses, with a rose leaf for a coverlet. There she slept at night, but in the daytime she played upon the table, where the woman had put a plate with a wreath of flowers around it, whose stalks stood in water. On the water swam a great tulip leaf, and on this the little maiden could sit and row from one side of the plate to the other, with two white horse hairs for oars. That looked pretty indeed! She could also sing so delicately and sweetly that nothing like it had ever been heard.

* * * * *

One night as she lay in her pretty bed, there came a Toad hopping in at the window through the broken glass. The Toad hopped straight down upon the table, where Thumbelina lay sleeping under the red rose leaf.

"That would be a handsome wife for my son," said the Toad, and she took the walnut shell in which Thumbelina lay asleep, and hopped with it through the window down into the garden.

There ran a great broad brook, with a swampy, soft bank, and here the Toad dwelt with her son. "Croak! Croak! Brek kek-kex!" That was all he could say when he saw the graceful little maiden in the walnut shell.

"Don't speak so loud, or she will awake," said the old Toad. "She might run away from us yet. We will put her out in the brook upon one of the broad water lily leaves. Out in the brook there grew many water lilies with broad green leaves, which looked as if they were floating on the water. The old Toad swam out to the largest one and laid on it the walnut shell with Thumbelina. The poor little thing woke early in the morning. There was water on every side of the great green leaf, and she could not get to land at all. Thumbelina began to cry.

The old Toad sat down in the mud, decking out her room with reeds and yellow water lilies—it was to be made very pretty for the new daughter-in-law. Then she swam out, with her son, to the leaf where Thumbelina was. The old Toad bowed before her in the water, and said, "Here is my son; he will be your husband, and you will live splendidly together in the mud."

"Croak! Croak! Brek-kek-kex!" was all the son could say.

Then they took the elegant little bed, and swam away with it, but Thumbelina sat all alone upon the green leaf and wept, for she did not want to have the Toad for a husband.

The little fishes swimming in the water below had both seen the Toad and looked up, for they wanted to see the little girl. As soon as they saw her they considered her so pretty that they felt very sorry she should have to marry the ugly Toad. No, that must never be! They assembled together in the water around the green stalk which held the leaf on which the little maiden stood, and with their teeth they gnawed away the stalk. And so the leaf swam down the stream. And away went Thumbelina far away, where the Toad could not get at her.

* * * * *

Thumbelina sailed by many places as she traveled out of the country, and the little birds which sat in the bushes saw her and said, "What a lovely little girl!"

A graceful little white Butterfly fluttered around her and at last alighted on the leaf. Thumbelina pleased him, and she was delighted, for now the Toad could not reach her. It was so beautiful where she was floating along—the sun shone upon the water like shining gold. She took her sash and tied one end of it around the Butterfly, fastening the other end of the ribbon to the leaf. The leaf now glided on much faster. Just then, a big Beetle flew up, and when he saw her he immediately clasped his claws around her slender waist and flew with her up into a tree. The green leaf went swimming down the brook, and the Butterfly with it; for he was fastened to the leaf, and could not get away from it.

Mercy! How frightened poor little Thumbelina was when the Beetle flew with her up into the tree! But she was especially sorry for the fine white Butterfly, for if he could not free himself from the leaf, he would starve to death. The Beetle, however, did not trouble himself at all about this. He seated himself with her upon the biggest green leaf of the tree, gave her the sweet part of the flowers to eat, and declared that she was very pretty, though she did not in the least resemble a beetle. Later, all the other beetles who lived in the tree came to pay a visit. The lady beetles shrugged their feelers and said, "Why, she only has two legs!—that looks terrible."

"She has no feelers!" cried another.

"Her waist is quite slender—my gracious! She looks like a human creature—how ugly she is!" said all the lady beetles.

And yet Thumbelina was very pretty. Even the Beetle who had carried her off thought so. But when all the others declared she was ugly, he believed it at last, and didn't want her at all. She was told she could go. They flew down with her from the tree and set her on a daisy, and she wept, because she thought she was so ugly that even the beetles didn't want her.

* * * * *

That whole summer poor Thumbelina lived quite alone in the great wood. She wove herself a bed out of blades of grass and hung it up under a large dandelion leaf, so that she was protected from the rain. She plucked the honey out of the flowers for food and drank of the dew which stood every morning upon the leaves. Thus summer turned to autumn and then to winter.

As Thumbelina wandered, she arrived at the door of the Field Mouse. This Mouse had a little hole under the stubble, where she

lived, warm and comfortable, and she had a whole room full of corn, a glorious kitchen, and a pantry. Poor Thumbelina stood at the door just like a poor beggar girl, and begged for a little bit of a barley-corn, for she had not had the smallest morsel to eat for the last two days.

"You poor little creature," said the Field Mouse—for after all she was a good old Field Mouse—"come into my warm room and dine with me."

As she was pleased with Thumbelina, she said, "If you like, you may stay with me through the winter, but you must keep my room clean and neat and tell me stories, for I am very fond of them."

And Thumbelina did as the kind old Field Mouse asked her and had a very good time of it.

"Now we shall soon have a visitor," said the Field Mouse. "My neighbor is in the habit of visiting me once a week. He is even better off than I am. If you could only get him for your husband you would be wealthy. But he cannot see at all. You must tell him the very best stories you know."

But Thumbelina did not care about this; she did not like the neighbor at all, for he was a mole. He came and paid his visits in his black velvet coat. The Field Mouse told how rich and how intelligent he was, and how his house was more than twenty times larger than hers. He had an education, but he did not like the sun and beautiful flowers, and said nasty things about them, for he had never seen them.

Thumbelina sang for him. Then the Mole fell in love with her because of her beautiful voice, but he said nothing, for he was a very serious man.

A short time before, he had dug a long passage through the earth from his own house to theirs, and Thumbelina and the Field Mouse were allowed to walk in this passage as much as they wished. But he begged them not to be afraid of the dead bird which was lying in the passage. It was an entire bird, with wings and a beak. It must have died only a short time before, when the winter began, and was now buried just where the Mole had made his passage. Thumbelina felt sorry for the bird which lay in the darkness of the tunnel.

* * * * *

One night Thumbelina could not sleep at all; so she got up out of her bed, and wove a large, beautiful carpet of hay, and carried it and spread it over the dead bird. She also laid soft cotton, which she had found in the Field Mouse's room, at the bird's sides, so that he might lie warm in the cold ground.

"Good-bye, pretty little bird!" said she. "Good-bye!" And then she laid her head on the bird's breast, but at once was greatly startled, for it felt as if something were beating inside. That was the bird's heart. The bird was not dead; he was only lying there stiff with cold, and now he had been warmed and come to life again.

Thumbelina fairly trembled, she was so startled; for the bird was large, very large, compared to a girl who was only an inch in height. But she took courage, laid the cotton closer round the poor bird, and brought a leaf of mint that she had used as her own coverlet, and laid it over the bird's head.

The next night she crept out to him again—and now he was alive, but quite weak. He could only open his eyes for a moment and look at Thumbelina, who stood before him with a bit of decayed wood in her hand, for she had no other lantern.

"I thank you, you pretty little child," said the sick Swallow. "I am warm now. Soon I shall get my strength back again, and I shall be able to fly about in the warm sunshine."

"Oh," she said, "it is so cold outside. It snows and freezes. Stay in your warm bed, and I will nurse you."

The whole winter the Swallow remained there, and Thumbelina nursed and tended him heartily. Neither the Field Mouse nor the Mole heard anything about it, for they did not like the poor Swallow. So soon as the spring came, and the sun warmed the earth, the Swallow told Thumbelina good-bye, and she helped him open a hole in the tunnel's ceiling. The sun shone in upon them gloriously, and the Swallow asked if Thumbelina would go with him; she could sit upon his back, and they would fly away far into the green wood. But Thumbelina knew that the old Field Mouse would be grieved if she left her.

"No, I cannot!" said Thumbelina.

"Good-bye, good-bye, you good, pretty girl!" said the Swallow, and he flew out into the sunshine. Thumbelina looked after him, and tears came into her eyes, for she liked the poor Swallow so much.

* * * * *

"Now you must work on making your clothes this summer," said the Field Mouse to her; for her neighbor, the tiresome Mole with the velvet coat, had proposed to Thumbelina. "You shall have woolen and linen clothes both; you will have everything you need when you become the Mole's wife."

Thumbelina had to turn the spindle, and the Mole hired four spiders to spin and weave for her day and night. Every evening the Mole paid her a visit, and he was always saying that when the summer should draw to a close, the sun would not shine nearly so hot, for now it burned the earth almost as hard as a stone. Yes, when the summer was over, then he would marry Thumbelina. But she was not glad at all, for she did not like the tiresome Mole.

"In four weeks you shall celebrate your wedding," said the Field Mouse to her.

But Thumbelina wept and declared she would not marry the tiresome Mole.

"Nonsense," said the Field Mouse.

Now the wedding was to be held. The Mole had already come to fetch Thumbelina; she was to live with him, deep under the earth, and never to come out into the warm sunshine that he did not like.

"Good-bye, bright sun!" she said, and stretched out her arms toward it, and walked a little way from the house of the Field Mouse, for now the corn had been reaped, and only the dry stubble stood in the fields. "Good-bye!" she repeated, and threw her little arms around a little red flower which still bloomed there. "Greet the dear Swallow from me, if you see him again."

"Tweet-weet! Tweet-weet!" a voice suddenly sounded over her head. She looked up, and it was the Swallow, who was just flying

by. When he saw Thumbelina he was very glad, and Thumbelina
told him how she didn't want to marry the ugly Mole and live deep
under the earth where the sun never shone. She could not help crying.

"The cold winter is coming now," said the Swallow. "I am going
to fly far away into the warm countries. Will you come with me?"

"Yes, I will go with you!" said Thumbelina, and she seated herself on the bird's back, with her feet on his outspread wings, and tied
her sash fast to one of his strongest feathers. Then the Swallow flew
up into the air over forest and over sea, high up over the great mountains, where the snow always lies. Thumbelina felt cold in the bleak
air, but then she crept under the bird's warm feathers, and only put
out her little head to admire all the beauties beneath her.

*   *   *   *   *

At last they came to the warm countries.

"Here is my house," said the Swallow. "But if you will select for
yourself one of the splendid flowers which grow down below, then

I will put you into it, and you shall have everything as nice as you could wish."

"That is wonderful," cried she, and clapped her little hands.

A great marble pillar lay there, which had fallen to the ground and had been broken into three pieces, but between these pieces grew the most beautiful great white flowers. The Swallow flew down with Thumbelina and set her upon one of the broad leaves. But how great was the little maid's surprise! There sat a little man in the midst of the flower, as white and transparent as if he had been made of glass. He wore the daintiest of gold crowns on his head, and the brightest wings on his shoulders; he himself was not bigger than Thumbelina. He was the Prince of the flower. In each of the flowers dwelt such a little prince, but this one was king over them all.

"How handsome he is!" whispered Thumbelina to the Swallow.

The little Prince was very much frightened at the Swallow; for it was quite a gigantic bird to him, who was so small. But when he saw Thumbelina, he became very glad; she was the prettiest maiden

he had ever seen. So he took off his golden crown and put it on her, asked her name, and if she would be his wife, and then she should be queen of all the flowers. Now this was truly a different kind of man from the son of the Toad, and the Mole with the black velvet fur. So, of course, she said yes to the charming Prince. And out of every flower came a lady or a lord, so pretty to see that it was a delight. Each one brought Thumbelina a present. The best gift was a pair of beautiful wings which had belonged to a great white fly; these were fastened to Thumbelina's back, and now she could fly from flower to flower. Then there was much rejoicing, and the Swallow sat above them in his nest, and sang to them.

"Good-bye, good-bye!" said the Swallow, and he flew away again from the warm countries, far away back to Denmark. There he has a little nest over the window of the man who can tell fairy tales. To him he sang, "Tweet-weet! Tweet-weet!" and from him we have the whole story.

THE WILD SWANS

This story is an excellent example of Paul's words to the Romans: "We also rejoice in our sufferings, because we know that suffering produces perseverance; perseverance, character; and character, hope." (Romans 5:3, 4) It also shows us the benefits of keeping our mouths shut!

ar away, where the swallows fly when our winter comes on, lived a King who had eleven sons and one daughter named Elisa. The eleven brothers were Princes, and each went to school with a star on his breast and his sword by his side. They wrote with pencils of diamond upon slates of gold and read aloud so well, one could see directly that they were Princes. Their sister Elisa sat upon a little stool made of mirrors and had a picture book which had been bought for the value of half a kingdom.

Oh, the children lived grandly, but it did not remain so.

Their father, who was King of the whole country, married an evil Queen who did not love the poor children at all.

The Queen took the little sister Elisa into the country to live with a peasant and his wife. Soon the Queen had told the King so many lies about the poor Princes that he did not care about them anymore.

"Fly out into the world and get your own living," said the wicked Queen. "Fly like great birds without a voice."

But she could not make it as bad for them as she would have liked, for they became eleven magnificent wild swans. With a strange cry, they flew out of the palace windows, far over the park and into the wood.

It was yet quite early morning when they came by the farm where their sister Elisa lay asleep in her room. Here they hovered over the roof, turned their long necks, and flapped their wings, but no one heard or saw it. They flew on into a great dark wood, which stretched away to the seashore.

Poor little Elisa sat in her room and played with a green leaf, for she had no other playthings. And she pricked a hole in the leaf and looked through it up at the sun, and it seemed to her that she saw her brothers' clear eyes. Each time the warm sun shone upon her cheeks, she thought of all the kisses they had given her.

When she was fifteen years old, Elisa was to go home. And when the Queen saw how beautiful she was, she became spiteful and filled with hatred toward her. She would have been glad to change her into a wild swan, like her brothers, but she did not dare to do so at once, because the King wished to see his daughter.

Early in the morning, the Queen went into the bath, which was built of white marble, and decked with soft cushions and the most splendid tapestry. She took three toads to scare Elisa, but when Elisa entered the tub, the toads became her friends rather than frightening her. She was too good and innocent for the toads to have done otherwise.

When the wicked Queen saw that, she rubbed Elisa with walnut juice, so that her skin became dirty. Then she smeared an evil-smelling ointment on her face and put ashes and dust in her beautiful hair. It was quite impossible to recognize the pretty Elisa.

When her father saw her, he was shocked and declared this was not his daughter. No one but the yard dog and the swallows recognized her, but they were only animals who had nothing to say in the matter.

Then poor Elisa wept and thought of her eleven brothers who were all away. Sorrowfully, she crept out of the castle and walked all day over field and moor till she came to the great wood. She did not know where she wished to go, she only knew she felt very downcast and longed for her brothers; they had certainly been, like herself, thrown into the world, and she would look for them and find them.

She had been in the wood only a short time when night fell. She quite lost the path, so she lay down upon the soft moss, said her evening prayer, and leaned her head against the stump of a tree.

The whole night long she dreamed of her brothers. When she awoke, the sun was already standing high. A number of springs flowed into a lake which had the most delightful sandy bottom. Here Elisa went down to the water.

When Elisa saw her own face in the lake she was terrified— so dirty and ugly was she, but when she wetted her little hand and rubbed her eyes and her forehead, her own skin gleamed forth again. After she had bathed in the fresh water, dressed herself again, and braided her long hair, Elisa went to the bubbling spring, drank out of her hand, and then wandered farther into the wood, not knowing where she went.

She thought of her dear brothers, and thought that God would certainly take care of all of them and herself, also. He showed her a wild apple tree, with the branches bending under the weight of the fruit. Here she had her midday meal and then went into the darkest part of the forest. There it was so still that she could hear her own footsteps, as well as the rustling of every dry leaf which crackled under her feet. Not one bird was to be seen; not one ray of sunlight could find its way through the great dark branches of the trees.

The night came on quite dark. Not a single glowworm now gleamed in the grass. Sadly, she lay down to sleep. Then it seemed to her that the branches of the trees parted above her head, and she knew that God was looking down on her, with angels looking over His shoulders.

* * * * *

The next morning Elisa went down the road and met an old woman with berries in her basket, and the old woman gave her a few of them. Elisa asked the woman if she had not seen eleven Princes riding through the wood.

"No," replied the old woman, "but yesterday I saw eleven swans swimming in the river close by, with golden crowns on their heads."

And she led Elisa a short distance farther, to a cliff, and at the foot of the slope a little river wound its way. Elisa said good-bye to the old woman and followed the river to where it flowed out to the great open ocean.

The whole glorious sea lay before the young girl's eyes, but not one sail appeared on its surface, and not a boat could be seen. How could she go on? She looked at the hundreds of little pebbles on the shore; the water had worn them all round. "It rolls on without getting tired, and thus what is hard becomes smooth. I won't get tired, either. Thanks for your lesson, you clear, rolling waves; my heart tells me that one day you will lead me to my dear brothers."

On the foam-covered sea grass lay eleven white swan feathers, which she collected into a bunch. Drops of water were upon them—whether they were dewdrops or tears, nobody could tell.

When the sun was just about to set, Elisa saw eleven wild swans, with crowns on their heads, flying toward the land. They swept along one after the other, so that they looked like a long, white band. Then Elisa climbed up the slope and hid herself behind a bush. The swans alighted near her and flapped their great white wings.

As soon as the sun had disappeared beneath the water, the swans' feathers fell off, and eleven handsome Princes stood there. She uttered a loud cry, for although they looked very different, she knew and felt that they must be her brothers. She sprang into their arms and called them by their names, and the Princes felt supremely happy when they saw their little sister again. They smiled and wept as they told of how cruel their stepmother had been to them all.

"We brothers," said the eldest, "fly about as wild swans as long as the sun is in the sky, but as soon as it sinks down, we receive our human form again. Therefore we must always take care that

we have a resting place for our feet when the sun sets; for if at that moment we were flying up toward the clouds, we would fall out of the sky as men."

"How can I break the spell?" asked the sister. And they talked nearly the whole night, only sleeping for a few hours.

*   *   *   *   *

She was awakened by the rustling of the swans' wings above her head. Her brothers were again enchanted, and they flew in wide circles and at last far away. But one of them, the youngest, remained behind, and the swan laid his head in her lap, and she stroked his wings, and the whole day they remained together. Toward evening the others came back, and when the sun had gone down they stood there in their own shapes.

"Tomorrow we fly far away from here and cannot come back until a whole year has gone by. But we cannot leave you like this! Do you have the courage to come with us? My arm is strong enough to carry you in the wood, and all our wings will be strong enough to fly with you over the sea."

"Yes, take me with you," said Elisa.

The whole night they stayed up weaving a net of the willow bark and tough reeds, and it was great and strong. On this net Elisa lay down, and when the sun rose, and her brothers were changed into wild swans, they seized the net with their beaks, and flew with their beloved sister, who was still asleep, high up toward the clouds. The sunbeams fell exactly upon her face, so one of the swans flew over her head, so that his broad wings might overshadow her.

They were far away from the shore when Elisa awoke; she thought she was still dreaming, so strange did it appear to her to be carried high through the air and over the sea. By her side lay a branch with beautiful ripe berries and a bundle of sweet-tasting roots. The youngest of the brothers had collected them and placed them there for her. She smiled at him thankfully, for she recognized him; he was the one flying over her and shading her with his wings.

The whole day they flew on through the air, like a whirring arrow, but their flight was slower than it should have been, for they had their sister to carry. Bad weather came on; the evening drew near. It seemed to her that the swans beat the air more strongly with their wings. Alas! She was the reason they could not fly fast enough. Then she prayed a prayer from the depths of her heart.

Now the sun just touched the edge of the sea. Elisa's heart trembled. Then the swans darted downward, so swiftly that she thought they were falling, but they paused again. The sun was half gone below the water. And now for the first time she saw a little rock beneath her, and it looked no larger than a seal might look, poking his head forth from the water. The sun sank very fast; at last it appeared only like a star. Then her foot touched the firm land. Her brothers were standing around her, arm in arm, but there was just enough room for her and for them. The sea beat against the rock and spilled over her like small rain; the sky glowed in continual fire, and crash upon crash the thunder rolled. But sister and brothers held each other by the hand and sang psalms, from which they gained comfort and courage.

In the morning twilight, the air was pure and calm. As soon as the sun rose, the swans flew away with Elisa from the island. When the sun mounted higher, Elisa saw before her the most glorious blue mountains, with cedar forests, cities, and palaces. Long before the sun went down, she sat on a rock in front of a great cave overgrown with delicate green trailing plants that looked like embroidered carpets.

"Now we shall see what you will dream of here tonight," said the youngest brother, and he showed her to her bedchamber.

"Heaven grant that I may dream of a way to set you free," she replied.

And she couldn't stop thinking about this, so she prayed for help, and even kept praying in her sleep.

Then she seemed to be flying high in the air. An angel came out to meet her, beautiful and radiant. Yet she was quite like the old woman who had given her the berries in the wood and had told her about the swans with golden crowns on their heads.

"Your brothers can be set free," said she. "But do you have courage and perseverance? Do you see the stinging nettle which I hold in my hand? Many of these same plants grow around the cave in which you sleep: only those will work. Those you must pluck, though they will burn your hands into blisters. Break these nettles to pieces with your feet, and you will have flax. From this you must weave eleven shirts of mail with long sleeves. Throw these over the eleven swans and they will become fully men again. But listen well— from

the moment you begin this work until it is finished, even if it should take years to accomplish, you must not speak. The first word you utter will pierce your brothers' hearts like a deadly dagger. Their lives depend on your tongue. Remember all this!"

Elisa passed the night at her work, for she could not sleep till she had saved her dear brothers. All the next day, while the swans were away, she sat alone, but never before had time flown so quickly. By evening, one shirt of mail was already finished, and she began the second.

* * * * *

The next day a hunting horn sounded among the hills, and Elisa was struck with fear. The noise came nearer and nearer. She heard the barking dogs and timidly she fled into the cave, bound into a bundle the nettles she had collected and prepared, and sat upon the bundle.

In only a few minutes, all the huntsmen stood before the cave, and the handsomest of them was the King of the country. When they saw that she had been weaving nettles, and that she would not speak, they were certain she was a witch. The King turned away, for he had never seen a more beautiful maiden.

"The people must judge her," said he.

And the people condemned her to suffer death by fire.

Elisa was led into a dark, damp cell where the wind whistled through the grated window. They gave her the bundle of nettles which she had collected. On this she could lay her head, and the hard, burning coats of mail which she had woven were to be her blanket. But nothing could have been given her that she liked better. She began her work again, weaving the shirts and praying to God.

But toward evening there came the whirring of swans' wings close by the grating—it was the youngest of her brothers. He had found his sister, and she sobbed aloud with joy. The work was almost finished, and her brothers were here.

The little mice ran about on the floor and dragged nettles to her feet in order to help her. The thrush perched beside the bars of the window and sang all night as merrily as it could, so that she might not lose heart.

An hour before sunrise, the eleven brothers stood at the castle gate and demanded to see the King. They were told they could not, for it was still almost night; the King was asleep and could not be disturbed. They begged and threatened and made enough noise that the sentries came, and yes, even the King himself came out, wanting to know the meaning of all this. At that moment the sun rose, and the eleven brothers disappeared, but eleven wild swans flew away over the castle.

All the people came flocking out at the town gate, for they wanted to see the girl burned as a witch. An old horse drew the cart on which Elisa sat. They had put upon her a garment of coarse sackcloth. Her lovely hair hung loose about her beautiful face. Her cheeks were as pale as death, and her lips moved silently, while her fingers were engaged with the green flax. Even on the way to death she did not interrupt the work she had begun. The ten shirts of mail lay at her feet, and she was praying as she wove the eleventh. The mob mocked her.

"Look at the girl, how she mutters!" They all pressed in on her and wanted to tear up the shirts of mail. Just then eleven wild swans came flying up and sat round about her on the cart and beat their wings. The mob backed away from them, terrified.

"That is a sign from heaven! She is certainly innocent!" whispered many. But they did not dare to say it aloud.

Finished at last, Elisa quickly threw the eleven shirts over the swans, and immediately eleven handsome Princes stood there. But the youngest had a swan's wing instead of an arm, for she had not quite finished one sleeve of his shirt.

"Now I may speak!" she said. "I am innocent!"

"Yes, she is innocent," said the eldest brother.

And now he told everything that had happened, and while he spoke, a fragrance arose like millions of roses, for every stick in the pile for the bonfire had taken root and was sending forth shoots. A fragrant hedge stood there, tall and great, covered with red roses, and at the top a white and shining flower gleamed like a star. This flower the King plucked and placed in Elisa's bosom, and she gazed on him with peace and happiness in her heart.

All the church bells rang by themselves, and the birds came in great flocks. And no King has ever seen a marriage procession happier than the one that now went back to the castle.

THE LOVELIEST ROSE IN THE WORLD

"This is how we know what love is: Jesus Christ laid down his life for us." (I John 3:16)

nce there reigned a Queen, in whose garden were found the most glorious flowers at all seasons and from all the lands in the world. The Queen especially loved roses. They grew against the castle walls, wound themselves round pillars and window frames, into the passages, and along the ceilings in the halls. The roses were various in fragrance, form, and color.

But care and sorrow dwelt in these halls; the Queen lay upon a sickbed, and the doctors declared that she would die.

"There is still one thing that can save her," said the wisest of them. "Bring her the loveliest rose in the world, the one which is the expression of the brightest and purest love, for if that is brought before her eyes, she will not die."

So young and old came from every side with roses, the loveliest that bloomed in each garden, but they were not the right sort. The flower had to be brought out of the garden of love, but which rose there expressed the highest and purest love?

The poets sang of the loveliest rose in the world, and each one named his own. Seekers were sent far round the land to every heart that beat with love, to every class and condition, and to every age.

"No one has till now named the flower," said the Wise Man. "No one has pointed out the place where it bloomed in its splendor."

"I know where it blooms," said a happy mother, who came with her child to the bedside of the Queen. The rose that is the expression of the highest and purest love springs from the blooming cheeks of my sweet child when she opens her eyes in the morning and smiles at me with all her affection!"

"This rose is lovely, but there is still one lovelier," said the Wise Man.

"Yes, a far lovelier one," said one of the women. "I have seen it, and a purer rose does not bloom. It was pale like the petals of the tea rose. I saw it on the cheeks of the Queen. She was carrying her sick child in her arms. She wept, kissed it, and prayed for her child as a mother prays in the darkest hour."

"Holy and wonderful in its might is the white rose of grief, but it is not the one we seek," said the Wise Man.

Then there came into the room a child, the Queen's little son. Tears stood in his eyes and glistened on his cheeks. He carried a great open book, and the binding was of velvet, with great silver clasps.

"Mother!" cried the little boy, "only hear what I have read."

And the child sat by the bedside and read from the book of Him who suffered death on the Cross to save men, and even those who were not yet born.

"Greater love has no one than this," he read, "that he lay down his life for his friends."

And a rose hue spread over the cheeks of the Queen, and her eyes gleamed, for she saw that from the leaves of the book there bloomed the loveliest rose, that sprang from the blood of Christ shed on the Cross.

"I see it!" she said, "he who beholds this, the loveliest rose on earth, shall never die."